Selected Stories by
SIR WALTER SCOTT

Books in this Series:

Selected Stories by O. Henry

Selected Stories by Anton Chekhov

Selected Stories by Guy de Maupassant

Selected Stories by Mark Twain

Selected Stories by Edgar Allan Poe

Selected Stories by Rudyard Kipling

Selected Stories by Saki

Selected Stories by Oscar Wilde

Selected Stories by Honoré de Balzac

Selected Stories by Charles Dickens

Selected Stories by D.H. Lawrence

Selected Stories by H.G. Wells

Selected Stories by Jack London

Selected Stories by Joseph Conrad

Selected Stories by Leo Tolstoy

Selected Stories by Sir Arthur Conan Doyle

Selected Stories by James Joyce

Selected Stories by Virginia Woolf

Selected Stories by Thomas Hardy

Selected Stories by Fyodor Dostoyevsky

Selected Stories by Katherine Mansfield

Selected Stories by Wilkie Collins

Selected Stories by Robert Louis Stevenson

Selected Stories by Howard Pyle

Selected Stories by Jerome K. Jerome

Selected Stories by H. Rider Haggard

Selected Stories by G.K. Chesterton

Selected Stories by
SIR WALTER SCOTT

RUPA

Published by
Rupa Publications India Pvt. Ltd 2015
7/16, Ansari Road, Daryaganj
New Delhi 110002

Sales Centres:
Allahabad Bengaluru Chennai
Hyderabad Jaipur Kathmandu
Kolkata Mumbai

Selection and Introduction copyright © Terry O'Brien 2015

All rights reserved.
No part of this publication may be reproduced, transmitted,
or stored in a retrieval system, in any form or by any means,
electronic, mechanical, photocopying, recording or otherwise,
without the prior permission of the publisher.

ISBN: 978-81-291-3687-9

First impression 2015

10 9 8 7 6 5 4 3 2 1

Printed at Shree Maitrey Printech Pvt. Ltd., Noida

This book is sold subject to the condition that it shall not,
by way of trade or otherwise, be lent, resold, hired out, or otherwise
circulated, without the publisher's prior consent, in any form of binding or
cover other than that in which it is published.

CONTENTS

Introduction   *vii*

1. My Aunt Margaret's Mirror   1
2. The Tapestried Chamber   40
3. Death of the Laird's Jock   58
4. Wandering Willie's Tale   65
5. The Two Drovers   88

INTRODUCTION

Born in Edinburgh, Scotland, Sir Walter Scott, first baronet, FRSE (15 August 1771–21 September 1832) was a novelist, historian, playwright, short-story writer, biographer, poet, critic and editor. Scott has also been considered by many to be the creator and the most active practitioner of the historical novel. Believed to be the first truly international author of his time, Scott had a dedicated and loyal readership in Europe, Australia and North America. He was an author who was avidly read, it is believed, by Karl Marx. His repertoire of works includes famous titles such as *Ivanhoe*, *Rob Roy*, *The Lady of the Lake*, *Waverley*, *The Heart of Midlothian* and *The Bride of Lammermoor*.

Scott may best be remembered for his novels and poems, but his short fiction, a format he experimented with, albeit minimally, cannot be forgotten. This even led some scholars to name him 'the father of the modern short story'.

Just like his novels and narrative poetry, Scott's short fiction features elements of Scottish folklore, legend and history, revealing aspects of the Scottish national character and often with some kind of supernatural, inexplicable event or circumstance at the core of the story.

This collection of short stories includes three which appeared in *The Keepsake for 1829*, a literary annual published for Christmas of 1828. The stories are 'My Aunt Margaret's Mirror', 'The Tapestried Chamber' and 'Death of the Laird's

Jock', which Scott together called *The Keepsake Stories*. The other two stories in this compilation are 'Wandering Willie's Tale' and 'The Two Drovers'. The latter was called 'the first modern short story in English' by literary critic and novelist Walter Allen, in a study of the short story that appeared in the 28 March 1974 issue of *The Listener*, a magazine started by the BBC in 1929.

- 'My Aunt Margaret's Mirror' is a story within a story, where Margaret, at the twilight of her life, narrates an incident to her nephew about a true event that took place in her ancestor, Lady Bothwell's life. Her sister, Lady Jemima, in a desperate bid to hear news about her husband who had volunteered to be part of an ongoing war, resolved to consult a doctor of questionable—and mysterious—abilities. What transpired is an astonishing revelation of betrayal, death and heartbreak, conveyed in the most unexpected way.
- 'The Tapestried Chamber' tells the story of a decorated war veteran who, on a visit to the country, chances upon a childhood friend and agrees to spend the night at his newly inherited mansion. The fantastic events that unfold over the night test even the intrepid soldier's bravery and make him question his sanity and his courage.
- In 'Death of the Laird's Jock' an invincible laird, extremely proud of his prodigious abilities with a two-handed sword and the streak of wins he notched up in his lifetime, is now laid up in bed. He is positive, however, that his son, set to battle an Englishman, will carry forward the baton of Scottish strength in a fight that has taken on great significance for father and son. It is a story where familial relationships are tested, and found wanting, at the altar of inconceivable pride.
- 'In Wandering Willie's Tale' a young student on a break from studies encounters a Scotsman and his wife and hears

a fantastical tale that seamlessly journeys between the real world and a phantasmagoria that closely resembles the netherworld. The Scotsman's seemingly true supernatural experiences and narrow escape from death become the highlight of that chance meeting.
- Set in the late eighteenth century, 'The Two Drovers' is a story of a Scotsman and an Englishman, drovers who found friendship over the long journeys they undertook to drive cattle across large distances. The two friends get into a fight over a perceived slight and a small misunderstanding, which puts their friendship to the ultimate test.

1

MY AUNT MARGARET'S MIRROR

'There are times
When Fancy plays her gambols, in despite
Even of our watchful senses—when in sooth
Substance seems shadow, shadow substance seems—
When the broad, palpable, and mark'd partition
'Twixt that which is and is not seems dissolved,
As if the mental eye gain'd power to gaze
Beyond the limits of the existing world.
Such hours of shadowy dreams I better love
Than all the gross realities of life.'

Anonymous

My Aunt Margaret was one of that respected sisterhood upon whom devolve all the trouble and solicitude incidental to the possession of children, excepting only that which attends their entrance into the world. We were a large family, of very different dispositions and constitutions. Some were dull and peevish—they were sent to Aunt Margaret to be amused; some were rude, romping, and boisterous—they were sent to Aunt Margaret to be kept quiet, or rather that their noise might be removed out of hearing; those who were indisposed were sent with the prospect of being nursed; those who were stubborn, with the hope of their being subdued by the kindness of Aunt Margaret's discipline;—in short, she had all the various duties of a mother, without the credit and dignity of the maternal character. The busy scene of her various cares is now over. Of the invalids and the robust, the kind and the rough, the peevish and pleased children, who thronged her little parlour from morning to night, not one now remains alive but myself, who, afflicted by early infirmity, was one of the most delicate of her nurslings, yet, nevertheless, have outlived them all.

It is still my custom, and shall be so while I have the use of my limbs, to visit my respected relation at least three times a week. Her abode is about half a mile from the suburbs of the town in which I reside, and is accessible, not only by the highroad, from which it stands at some distance, but by means of a greensward footpath leading through some pretty meadows. I have so little left to torment me in life, that it is one of my greatest vexations to know that several of these sequestered fields have been devoted as sites for building. In that which is nearest the town, wheelbarrows have been at work for several weeks in such numbers, that, I verily believe, its whole surface, to the depth of at least eighteen inches, was mounted in these monotrochs at the same moment, and in the act of being transported from one place to another. Huge triangular piles of planks are also reared in different parts of the devoted messuage; and a little group of trees that still grace the eastern end, which rises in a gentle ascent, have just received warning to quit, expressed by a daub of white paint, and are to give place to a curious grove of chimneys.

It would, perhaps, hurt others in my situation to reflect that this little range of pasturage once belonged to my father (whose family was of some consideration in the world), and was sold by patches to remedy distresses in which he involved himself in an attempt by commercial adventure to redeem his diminished fortune. While the building scheme was in full operation, this circumstance was often pointed out to me by the class of friends who are anxious that no part of your misfortunes should escape your observation. 'Such pasture-ground!—lying at the very town's end—in turnips and potatoes, the parks would bring L20 per acre; and if leased for building—oh, it was a gold mine! And all sold for an old song out of the ancient possessor's hands!' My comforters cannot bring me to repine much on this subject. If I could be allowed to look back on the past without interruption, I could willingly give up the enjoyment of present income and the hope of future profit to those who have purchased what my father sold. I regret the alteration of the ground only because it destroys associations, and I would more willingly (I think) see the Earl's Closes in the hands of strangers, retaining their silvan appearance, than know them for my own, if torn up by agriculture, or covered with buildings. Mine are the sensations of poor Logan:

'The horrid plough has rased the green
Where yet a child I strayed;
The axe has fell'd the hawthorn screen,
The schoolboy's summer shade.'

I hope, however, the threatened devastation will not be consummated in my day. Although the adventurous spirit of times short while since passed gave rise to the undertaking, I have been encouraged to think that the subsequent changes have so far damped the spirit of speculation that the rest of the woodland footpath leading to Aunt Margaret's retreat will be left undisturbed for her time and mine. I am interested in this, for every step of the way, after I have passed through the green already mentioned, has for me something of early remembrance:—There is the stile at which I can recollect a cross child's-maid upbraiding me with my infirmity as she lifted me coarsely and carelessly over the flinty steps, which my brothers traversed with shout and bound. I remember the suppressed bitterness of the moment, and, conscious of my own inferiority, the feeling of envy with which I regarded the easy movements and elastic steps of my more happily formed brethren. Alas! these goodly barks have all perished on life's wide ocean, and only that which seemed so little seaworthy, as the naval phrase goes, has reached the port when the tempest is over. Then there is the pool, where, manoeuvring our little navy, constructed out of the broad water-flags, my elder brother fell in, and was scarce saved from the watery element to die under Nelson's banner. There is the hazel copse also, in which my brother Henry used to gather nuts, thinking little that he was to die in an Indian jungle in quest of rupees.

There is so much more of remembrance about the little walk, that—as I stop, rest on my crutch-headed cane, and look round with that species of comparison between the thing I was and that which I now am—it almost induces me to doubt my own identity; until I find myself in face of the honeysuckle porch of Aunt Margaret's dwelling, with its irregularity of front, and its odd, projecting latticed windows, where the workmen seem to have made it a study that no one of them should resemble another in form, size, or in the old-fashioned stone entablature and labels which adorn them. This tenement, once the manor house of the Earl's Closes, we still retain a slight hold upon; for, in some family arrangements, it had been settled upon Aunt Margaret during the term of her life. Upon this frail tenure depends, in a great measure, the last shadow of the family of Bothwell of Earl's Closes, and their last slight connection with their paternal inheritance. The only representative will then be an infirm old man, moving not unwillingly to the grave, which has devoured all that were dear to his affections.

When I have indulged such thoughts for a minute or two, I enter the mansion, which is said to have been the gate-house only of the original building, and find one being on whom time seems to have made little impression; for the Aunt Margaret of to-day bears the same proportional age to the Aunt Margaret of my early youth that the boy of ten years old does to the man of (by'r Lady!) some fifty-six years. The old lady's invariable costume has doubtless some share in confirming one in the opinion that time has stood still with Aunt Margaret.

The brown or chocolate-coloured silk gown, with ruffles of the same stuff at the elbow, within which are others of Mechlin lace; the black silk gloves, or mitts; the white hair combed back upon a roll; and the cap of spotless cambric, which closes around the venerable countenance—as they were not the costume of 1780, so neither were they that of 1826; they are altogether a style peculiar to the individual Aunt Margaret. There she still sits, as she sat thirty years since, with her wheel or the stocking, which she works by the fire in winter and by the window in summer; or, perhaps, venturing as far as the porch in an unusually fine summer evening. Her frame, like some well-constructed piece of mechanics, still performs the operations for which it had seemed destined—going its round with an activity which is gradually diminished, yet indicating no probability that it will soon come to a period.

The solicitude and affection which had made Aunt Margaret the willing slave to the inflictions of a whole nursery, have now for their object the health and comfort of one old and infirm man—the last remaining relative of her family, and the only one who can still find interest in the traditional stores which she hoards, as some miser hides the gold which he desires that no one should enjoy after his death.

My conversation with Aunt Margaret generally relates little either to the present or to the future. For the passing day we possess as much as we require, and we neither of us wish for more; and for that which is to follow, we have, on this side of the grave, neither hopes, nor fears, nor anxiety. We therefore naturally look back to the past, and forget the present fallen fortunes and declined importance of our family in recalling the hours when it was wealthy and prosperous.

With this slight introduction, the reader will know as much of Aunt Margaret and her nephew as is necessary to comprehend the following conversation and narrative.

Last week, when, late in a summer evening, I went to call on the old lady to whom my reader is now introduced, I was received by her with all her usual affection and benignity, while, at the same time, she seemed abstracted and disposed to silence. I asked her the reason. 'They have been clearing out the old chapel,' she said; 'John Clayhudgeons having, it seems, discovered that the stuff within—being, I suppose, the remains of our ancestors—was excellent for top-dressing the meadows.'

Here I started up with more alacrity than I have displayed for some years; but sat down while my aunt added, laying her hand upon my sleeve, 'The chapel has been long considered as common ground, my dear, and used for a pinfold, and what objection can we have to the man for employing what is his own to his own profit? Besides, I did speak to him, and he very readily and civilly promised that if he found bones or monuments, they should be carefully respected and reinstated; and what more could I ask? So, the first stone they found bore the name of Margaret Bothwell, 1585, and I have caused it to be laid carefully aside, as I think it betokens death, and having served my namesake two hundred years, it has just been cast up in time to do me the same good turn. My house has been long put in order, as far as the small earthly concerns require it; but who shall say that their account with, Heaven is sufficiently revised?'

'After what you have said, aunt,' I replied, 'perhaps I ought to take my hat and go away; and so I should, but that there is on this occasion a little alloy mingled with your devotion. To think of death at all times is a duty—to suppose it nearer from the finding an old gravestone is superstition; and you, with your strong, useful common sense, which was so long the prop of a fallen family, are the last person whom I should have suspected of such weakness.'

'Neither would I deserve your suspicions, kinsman,' answered Aunt Margaret, 'if we were speaking of any incident occurring in the actual business of human life. But for all this, I have a sense of superstition about me, which I do not wish to part with. It is a feeling which separates me from this age, and links me with that to which I am hastening; and even when it seems, as now, to lead me to the brink of the grave, and bid me gaze on it, I do not love that it should be dispelled. It soothes my imagination, without influencing my reason or conduct.'

'I profess, my good lady,' replied I, 'that had any one but you made such a declaration, I should have thought it as capricious as that of the clergyman, who, without vindicating his false reading, preferred, from habit's sake, his old Mumpsimus to the modern Sumpsimus.'

'Well,' answered my aunt, 'I must explain my inconsistency in this particular by comparing it to another. I am, as you know, a piece of that old-fashioned thing called a Jacobite; but I am so in sentiment and feeling only, for a more loyal subject never joined in prayers for the health and wealth of George the Fourth, whom God long preserve! But I dare say that kind-hearted sovereign would not deem that an old woman did him much injury if she leaned back in her arm-chair, just in such a twilight as this, and thought of the high-mettled men whose sense of duty called them to arms against his grandfather; and how, in a cause which they deemed that of their rightful prince and country,

"They fought till their hand to the broadsword was glued,
They fought against fortune with hearts unsubdued."

Do not come at such a moment, when my head is full of plaids, pibrochs, and claymores, and ask my reason to admit what, I am afraid, it cannot deny—I mean, that the public advantage peremptorily demanded that these things should cease to exist. I cannot, indeed, refuse to allow the justice of your reasoning; but yet, being convinced against my will, you will gain little by your motion. You might as well read to an infatuated lover the catalogue of his mistress's imperfections; for when he has been compelled to listen to the summary, you will only get for answer that 'he lo'es her a' the better.'

I was not sorry to have changed the gloomy train of Aunt Margaret's thoughts, and replied in the same tone, 'Well, I can't help being persuaded that our good King is the more sure of Mrs Bothwell's loyal affection, that he has the Stewart right of birth as well as the Act of Succession in his favour.'

'Perhaps my attachment, were its source of consequence, might be found warmer for the union of the rights you mention,' said Aunt Margaret; 'but, upon my word, it would be as sincere if the King's right were founded only on the will of the nation, as declared at the Revolution. I am none of your JURE DIVINO folks.'

'And a Jacobite notwithstanding.'

'And a Jacobite notwithstanding—or rather, I will give you leave to call me one of the party which, in Queen Anne's time, were called, WHIMSICALS, because they were sometimes operated upon by feelings, sometimes by principle. After all, it is very hard that you will not allow an old woman to be as inconsistent in her political sentiments as mankind in general show themselves in all the various courses of life; since you cannot point out one of them in which the passions and prejudices of those who pursue it are not perpetually carrying us away from the path which our reason points out.'

'True, aunt; but you are a wilful wanderer, who should be forced back into the right path.'

'Spare me, I entreat you,' replied Aunt Margaret. 'You remember the Gaelic song, though I dare say I mispronounce the words—

"Hatil mohatil, na dowski mi."

(I am asleep, do not waken me.)

I tell you, kinsman, that the sort of waking dreams which my imagination spins out, in what your favourite Wordsworth calls "moods of my own mind," are worth all the rest of my more active days. Then, instead of looking forwards, as I did in youth, and forming for myself fairy palaces, upon the verge of the grave I turn my eyes backward upon the days and manners of my better time; and the sad, yet soothing recollections come so close and interesting, that I almost think it sacrilege to be wiser or more rational or less prejudiced than those to whom I looked up in my younger years.'

'I think I now understand what you mean,' I answered, 'and can comprehend why you should occasionally prefer the twilight of illusion to the steady light of reason.'

'Where there is no task,' she rejoined, 'to be performed, we may sit in the dark if we like it; if we go to work, we must ring for candles.'

'And amidst such shadowy and doubtful light,' continued I, 'imagination frames her enchanted and enchanting visions, and sometimes passes them upon the senses for reality.'

'Yes,' said Aunt Margaret, who is a well-read woman, 'to those who resemble the translator of Tasso,—

"Prevailing poet, whose undoubting mind
Believed the magic wonders which he sung."

It is not required for this purpose that you should be sensible of the painful horrors which an actual belief in such prodigies inflicts. Such a belief nowadays belongs only to fools and children. It is not necessary that your ears should tingle and your complexion change, like that of Theodore at the approach of the spectral huntsman. All that is indispensable for the enjoyment of the milder feeling of supernatural awe is, that you should be susceptible of the slight shuddering which creeps over you when you hear a tale of terror—that well-vouched tale which the narrator, having first expressed his general disbelief of all such legendary lore, selects and produces, as having something in it which he has been always obliged to give up as inexplicable. Another symptom is a momentary hesitation to look round you, when the interest of the narrative is at the highest; and the third, a desire to avoid looking into a mirror when you are alone in your chamber for the evening. I mean such are signs which indicate the crisis, when a female imagination is in due temperature to enjoy a ghost story. I do not pretend to describe those which express the same disposition in a gentleman.'

'That last symptom, dear aunt, of shunning the mirror seems likely to be a rare occurrence amongst the fair sex.'

'You are a novice in toilet fashions, my dear cousin. All women consult the looking-glass with anxiety before they go into company; but when they return home, the mirror has not the same charm. The die has been cast—the party has been successful or unsuccessful in the impression which she desired to make. But, without going deeper into the mysteries of the dressing-table, I will tell you that I myself, like many other honest folks, do not like to see the blank, black front of a large mirror in a room dimly lighted, and where the reflection of the candle seems rather to lose itself in the deep obscurity of the glass than to be reflected back again into the apartment. That space of inky darkness seems to be a field for Fancy to play her revels in. She may call up other features to meet us, instead of the reflection of our own; or, as in the spells of Hallowe'en, which we learned in childhood, some unknown form may be seen peeping over our shoulder. In short, when I am in a ghost-seeing humour, I make my handmaiden draw the green curtains over the mirror before I go into the room, so that she may have the first shock of the apparition, if there be any to be seen, But, to tell you the truth, this dislike to look into a mirror in particular times and places has, I believe, its original foundation in a story which came to me by tradition from my grandmother, who was a party concerned in the scene of which I will now tell you.'

THE MIRROR.

You are fond (said my aunt) of sketches of the society which has passed away. I wish I could describe to you Sir Philip Forester, the 'chartered libertine' of Scottish good company, about the end of the last century. I never saw him indeed; but my mother's traditions were full of his wit, gallantry, and dissipation. This gay knight flourished about the end of the seventeenth and beginning of the eighteenth century. He was the Sir Charles Easy and the Lovelace of his day and country—renowned for the number of duels he had fought, and the successful intrigues which he had carried on. The supremacy which he had attained in the fashionable world was absolute; and when we combine it with one or two anecdotes, for which, 'if laws were made for every degree,' he ought certainly to have been hanged, the popularity of such a person really serves to show, either that the present times are much more decent, if not more virtuous, than they formerly were, or that high-breeding then was of more difficult attainment than that which is now so called, and consequently entitled the successful professor to a proportional degree of plenary indulgences and privileges. No beau of this day could have borne out so ugly a story as that of Pretty Peggy Grindstone, the miller's daughter at Sillermills—it had well-nigh made work for the Lord Advocate. But it hurt Sir Philip Forester no more than the hail hurts the hearthstone. He was as well received in society as ever, and dined with the Duke of A—the day the poor girl was buried. She died of heartbreak. But that has nothing to do with my story.

Now, you must listen to a single word upon kith, kin, and ally; I promise you I will not be prolix. But it is necessary to the authenticity of my legend that you should know that Sir Philip Forester, with his handsome person, elegant accomplishments, and fashionable manners, married the younger Miss Falconer of King's Copland. The elder sister of this lady had previously become the wife of my grandfather, Sir Geoffrey Bothwell, and brought into our family a good fortune. Miss Jemima, or Miss Jemmie Falconer, as she was usually called, had also about ten thousand pounds sterling—then thought a very handsome portion indeed.

The two sisters were extremely different, though each had their admirers while they remained single. Lady Bothwell had some touch of the old King's Copland blood about her. She was bold, though not to the degree of audacity, ambitious, and desirous to raise her house and family; and was, as has been said, a considerable spur to my grandfather, who was otherwise an indolent man, but whom, unless he has been slandered, his lady's influence involved in some political matters which had been more wisely let alone. She was a woman of high principle, however, and masculine good sense, as some of her letters testify, which are still in my wainscot cabinet.

Jemmie Falconer was the reverse of her sister in every respect. Her understanding did not reach above the ordinary pitch, if, indeed, she could be said to have attained it. Her beauty, while it lasted, consisted, in a great measure, of delicacy of complexion and regularity of features, without any peculiar force of expression. Even these charms faded under the sufferings attendant on an ill-assorted match. She was passionately attached to her husband, by whom she was treated with a callous yet polite indifference, which, to one whose heart was as tender as her judgment was weak, was more painful perhaps than absolute ill-usage. Sir Philip was a voluptuary—that is, a completely selfish egotist—whose disposition and character resembled the rapier he wore, polished, keen, and brilliant, but inflexible and unpitying. As he observed carefully all the usual forms towards his lady, he had the art to deprive her even of the compassion of the world; and useless and unavailing as that may be while actually possessed by the sufferer, it is, to a mind like Lady Forester's, most painful to know she has it not.

The tattle of society did its best to place the peccant husband above the suffering wife. Some called her a poor, spiritless thing, and declared that, with a little of her sister's spirit, she might have brought to reason any Sir Philip whatsoever, were it the termagant Falconbridge himself. But the greater part of their acquaintance affected candour, and saw faults on both sides—though, in fact, there only existed the oppressor and the oppressed. The tone of such critics was, 'To be sure, no one will justify Sir Philip Forester, but then we all know Sir Philip, and Jemmie Falconer might have known what she had to expect from the beginning. What made her set her cap at Sir Philip? He would never have looked at her if she had not thrown herself at his head, with her poor ten thousand pounds. I am sure, if it is money he wanted, she spoiled his market. I know where Sir Philip could have done much better. And then, if she WOULD have the man, could not she try to make him more comfortable at home, and have his friends oftener, and not plague him with the squalling children, and take care all was handsome and in good style about the house? I declare I think Sir Philip would have made a very domestic man, with a woman who knew how to manage him.'

Now these fair critics, in raising their profound edifice of domestic felicity, did not recollect that the corner-stone was wanting, and that to receive good company with good cheer, the means of the banquet ought to have been furnished by Sir Philip, whose income (dilapidated as it was) was not equal to the display of the hospitality required, and at the same time to the supply of the good knight's MENUS PLAISIRS. So, in spite of all that was so sagely suggested by female friends, Sir Philip carried his good-humour everywhere abroad, and left at home a solitary mansion and a pining spouse.

At length, inconvenienced in his money affairs, and tired even of the short time which he spent in his own dull house, Sir Philip Forester determined to take a trip to the Continent, in the capacity of a volunteer. It was then common for men of fashion to do so; and our knight perhaps was of opinion that a touch of the military character, just enough to exalt, but not render pedantic, his qualities as a BEAU GARCON, was necessary to maintain possession of the elevated situation which he held in the ranks of fashion.

Sir Philip's resolution threw his wife into agonies of terror; by which the worthy baronet was so much annoyed, that, contrary to his wont, he took some trouble to soothe her apprehensions, and once more brought her to shed tears, in which sorrow was not altogether unmingled with pleasure. Lady Bothwell asked, as a favour, Sir Philip's permission to receive her sister and her family into her own house during his absence on the Continent. Sir Philip readily assented to a proposition which saved expense, silenced the foolish people who might have talked of a deserted wife and family, and gratified Lady Bothwell, for whom he felt some respect, as for one who often spoke to him, always with freedom and sometimes with severity, without being deterred either by his raillery or the PRESTIGE of his reputation.

A day or two before Sir Philip's departure, Lady Bothwell took the liberty of asking him, in her sister's presence, the direct question, which his timid wife had often desired, but never ventured, to put to him:—

'Pray, Sir Philip, what route do you take when you reach the Continent?'

'I go from Leith to Helvoet by a packet with advices.'

'That I comprehend perfectly,' said Lady Bothwell dryly; 'but you do not mean to remain long at Helvoet, I presume, and I should like to know what is your next object.'

'You ask me, my dear lady,' answered Sir Philip, 'a question which I have not dared to ask myself. The answer depends on the fate of war. I shall, of course, go to headquarters, wherever they may happen to be for the time; deliver my letters of introduction; learn as much of the noble art of war as may suffice a poor interloping amateur; and then take a glance at the sort of thing of which we read so much in the Gazette.'

'And I trust, Sir Philip,' said Lady Bothwell, 'that you will remember that you are a husband and a father; and that, though you think fit to indulge this military fancy, you will not let it hurry you into dangers which it is certainly unnecessary for any save professional persons to encounter.'

'Lady Bothwell does me too much honour,' replied the adventurous knight, 'in regarding such a circumstance with the slightest interest. But to soothe your flattering anxiety, I trust your ladyship will recollect that I cannot expose to hazard the venerable and paternal character which you so obligingly recommend to my protection, without putting in some peril an honest fellow, called Philip Forester, with whom I have kept company for thirty years, and with whom, though some folks consider him a coxcomb, I have not the least desire to part.'

'Well, Sir Philip, you are the best judge of your own affairs. I have little right to interfere—you are not my husband.'

'God forbid!' said Sir Philip hastily; instantly adding, however, 'God forbid that I should deprive my friend Sir Geoffrey of so inestimable a treasure.'

'But you are my sister's husband,' replied the lady; 'and I suppose you are aware of her present distress of mind—'

'If hearing of nothing else from morning to night can make me aware of it,' said Sir Philip, 'I should know something of the matter.'

'I do not pretend to reply to your wit, Sir Philip,' answered Lady Bothwell; 'but you must be sensible that all this distress is on account of apprehensions for your personal safety.'

'In that case, I am surprised that Lady Bothwell, at least, should give herself so much trouble upon so insignificant a subject.'

'My sister's interest may account for my being anxious to learn something of Sir Philip Forester's motions; about which, otherwise, I know he would not wish me to concern myself. I have a brother's safety too to be anxious for.'

'You mean Major Falconer, your brother by the mother's side? What can he possibly have to do with our present agreeable conversation?'

'You have had words together, Sir Philip,' said Lady Bothwell.

'Naturally; we are connections,' replied Sir Philip, 'and as such have always had the usual intercourse.'

'That is an evasion of the subject,' answered the lady. 'By words, I mean angry words, on the subject of your usage of your wife.'

'If,' replied Sir Philip Forester, 'you suppose Major Falconer simple enough to intrude his advice upon me, Lady Bothwell, in my domestic matters, you are indeed warranted in believing that I might possibly be so far displeased with the interference as to request him to reserve his advice till it was asked.'

'And being on these terms, you are going to join the very army in which my brother Falconer is now serving?'

'No man knows the path of honour better than Major Falconer,' said Sir Philip. 'An aspirant after fame, like me, cannot choose a better guide than his footsteps.'

Lady Bothwell rose and went to the window, the tears gushing from her eyes.

'And this heartless raillery,' she said, 'is all the consideration that is to be given to our apprehensions of a quarrel which may bring on the most terrible consequences? Good God! of what can men's hearts be made, who can thus dally with the agony of others?'

Sir Philip Forester was moved; he laid aside the mocking tone in which he had hitherto spoken.

'Dear Lady Bothwell,' he said, taking her reluctant hand, 'we are both wrong. You are too deeply serious; I, perhaps, too little so. The dispute I had with Major Falconer was of no earthly consequence. Had anything occurred betwixt us that ought to have been settled PAR VOIE DU FAIT, as we say in France, neither of us are persons that are likely to postpone such a meeting. Permit me to say, that were it generally known that you or my Lady Forester are apprehensive of such a catastrophe, it might be the very means of bringing about what would not otherwise be likely to happen. I know your good sense, Lady Bothwell, and that you will understand me when I say that really my affairs require my absence for some months. This Jemima cannot understand. It is a perpetual recurrence of questions, why can you not do this, or that, or the third thing? and, when you have proved to her that her expedients are totally ineffectual, you have just to begin the whole round again. Now, do you tell her, dear Lady Bothwell, that YOU are satisfied. She is, you must confess, one of those persons with whom authority goes farther than reasoning. Do but repose a little confidence in me, and you shall see how amply I will repay it.'

Lady Bothwell shook her head, as one but half satisfied. 'How difficult it is to extend confidence, when the basis on which it ought to rest has been so much shaken! But I will do my best to make Jemima easy; and further, I can only say that for keeping your present purpose I hold you responsible both to God and man,'

'Do not fear that I will deceive you,' said Sir Philip. 'The safest conveyance to me will be through the general post-office, Helvoetsluys, where I will take care to leave orders for forwarding my letters. As for Falconer, our only encounter will be over a bottle of Burgundy; so make yourself perfectly easy on his score.'

Lady Bothwell could NOT make herself easy; yet she was sensible that her sister hurt her own cause by TAKING ON, as the maidservants call it, too vehemently, and by showing before every stranger, by manner, and sometimes by words also, a dissatisfaction with her husband's journey that was sure to come to his ears, and equally certain to displease him. But there was no help for this domestic dissension, which ended only with the day of separation.

I am sorry I cannot tell, with precision, the year in which Sir Philip Forester went over to Flanders; but it was one of those in which the campaign opened with extraordinary fury, and many bloody, though indecisive, skirmishes were fought between the French on the one side and the Allies on the other. In all our modern improvements, there are none, perhaps, greater than in the accuracy and speed with which intelligence is transmitted from any scene of action to those in this country whom it may concern. During Marlborough's campaigns, the sufferings of the many who had relations in, or along with, the army were greatly augmented by the suspense in which they were detained for weeks after they had heard of bloody battles, in which, in all probability, those for whom their bosoms throbbed with anxiety had been personally engaged. Amongst those who were most agonized by this state of uncertainty was the—I had almost said deserted—wife of the gay Sir Philip Forester. A single letter had informed her of his arrival on the Continent; no others were received. One notice occurred in the newspapers, in which Volunteer Sir Philip Forester was mentioned as having been entrusted with a dangerous reconnaissance, which he had executed with the greatest courage, dexterity, and intelligence, and received the thanks of the commanding officer. The sense of his having acquired distinction brought a momentary glow into the lady's pale cheek; but it was instantly lost in ashen whiteness at the recollection of his danger. After this, they had no news whatever, neither from Sir Philip, nor even from their brother Falconer. The case of Lady Forester was not indeed different from that of hundreds in the same situation; but a feeble mind is necessarily an irritable one, and the suspense which some bear with constitutional indifference or philosophical resignation, and some with a disposition to believe and hope the best, was intolerable to Lady Forester, at once solitary and sensitive, low-spirited, and devoid of strength of mind, whether natural or acquired.

As she received no further news of Sir Philip, whether directly or indirectly, his unfortunate lady began now to feel a sort of consolation even in those careless habits which had so often given her pain. 'He is so thoughtless,' she repeated a hundred times a day to her sister, 'he never writes when things are going on smoothly. It is his way. Had anything happened, he would have informed us.'

Lady Bothwell listened to her sister without attempting to console her. Probably she might be of opinion that even the worst intelligence which could be received from Flanders might not be without some touch of consolation; and that the Dowager Lady Forester, if so she was doomed to be called, might have a source of happiness unknown to the wife of the gayest and finest gentleman in Scotland. This conviction became stronger as they learned from inquiries made at headquarters that Sir Philip was no longer with the army—though whether he had been taken or slain in some of those skirmishes which were perpetually occurring, and in which he loved to distinguish himself, or whether he had, for some unknown reason or capricious change of mind, voluntarily left the service, none of his countrymen in the camp of the Allies could form even a conjecture. Meantime his creditors at home became clamorous, entered into possession of his property, and threatened his person, should he be rash enough to return to Scotland. These additional disadvantages aggravated Lady Bothwell's displeasure against the fugitive husband; while her sister saw nothing in any of them, save what tended to increase her grief for the absence of him whom her imagination now represented—as it had before marriage—gallant, gay, and affectionate.

About this period there appeared in Edinburgh a man of singular appearance and pretensions. He was commonly called the Paduan Doctor, from having received his education at that famous university. He was supposed to possess some rare receipts in medicine, with which, it was affirmed, he had wrought remarkable cures. But though, on the one hand, the physicians of Edinburgh termed him an empiric, there were many persons, and among them some of the clergy, who, while they admitted the truth of the cures and the force of his remedies, alleged that Doctor Baptista Damiotti made use of charms and unlawful arts in order to obtain success in his practice. The resorting to him was even solemnly preached against, as a seeking of health from idols, and a trusting to the help which was to come from Egypt. But the protection which the Paduan Doctor received from some friends of interest and consequence enabled him to set these imputations at defiance, and to assume, even in the city of Edinburgh, famed as it was for abhorrence of witches and necromancers, the dangerous character of an expounder of futurity. It was at length rumoured that, for a certain gratification, which of course was not an inconsiderable one, Doctor Baptista Damiotti could tell the fate of the absent, and even show his visitors the personal form of their absent friends, and the action in which they were engaged at the moment. This rumour came to the ears of Lady Forester, who had reached that pitch of mental agony in which the sufferer will do anything, or endure anything, that suspense may be converted into certainty.

Gentle and timid in most cases, her state of mind made her equally obstinate and reckless, and it was with no small surprise and alarm that her sister, Lady Bothwell, heard her express a resolution to visit this man of art, and learn from him the fate of her husband. Lady Bothwell remonstrated on the improbability that such pretensions as those of this foreigner could be founded in anything but imposture.

'I care not,' said the deserted wife, 'what degree of ridicule I may incur; if there be any one chance out of a hundred that I may obtain some certainty of my husband's fate, I would not miss that chance for whatever else the world can offer me.'

Lady Bothwell next urged the unlawfulness of resorting to such sources of forbidden knowledge.

'Sister,' replied the sufferer, 'he who is dying of thirst cannot refrain from drinking even poisoned water. She who suffers under suspense must seek information, even were the powers which offer it unhallowed and infernal. I go to learn my fate alone, and this very evening will I know it; the sun that rises to-morrow shall find me, if not more happy, at least more resigned.'

'Sister,' said Lady Bothwell, 'if you are determined upon this wild step, you shall not go alone. If this man be an impostor, you may be too much agitated by your feelings to detect his villainy. If, which I cannot believe, there be any truth in what he pretends, you shall not be exposed alone to a communication of so extraordinary a nature. I will go with you, if indeed you determine to go. But yet reconsider your project, and renounce inquiries which cannot be prosecuted without guilt, and perhaps without danger.'

Lady Forester threw herself into her sister's arms, and, clasping her to her bosom, thanked her a hundred times for the offer of her company, while she declined with a melancholy gesture the friendly advice with which it was accompanied.

When the hour of twilight arrived—which was the period when the Paduan Doctor was understood to receive the visits of those who came to consult with him—the two ladies left their apartments in the Canongate of Edinburgh, having their dress arranged like that of women of an inferior description, and their plaids disposed around their faces as they were worn by the same class; for in those days of aristocracy the quality of the wearer was generally indicated by the manner in which her plaid was disposed, as well as by the fineness of its texture. It was Lady Bothwell who had suggested this species of disguise, partly to avoid observation as they should go to the conjurer's house, and partly in order to make trial of his penetration, by appearing before him in a feigned character. Lady Forester's servant, of tried fidelity, had been employed by her to propitiate the Doctor by a suitable fee, and a story intimating that a soldier's wife desired to know the fate of her husband—a subject upon which, in all probability, the sage was very frequently consulted.

To the last moment, when the palace clock struck eight, Lady Bothwell earnestly watched her sister, in hopes that she might retreat from her rash undertaking; but as mildness, and even timidity, is capable at times of vehement and fixed purposes, she found Lady Forester resolutely unmoved and determined when the moment of departure arrived. Ill satisfied with the expedition, but determined not to leave her sister at such a crisis, Lady Bothwell accompanied Lady Forester through more than one obscure street and lane, the servant walking before, and acting as their guide. At length he suddenly turned into a narrow court, and knocked at an arched door which seemed to belong to a building of some antiquity. It opened, though no one appeared to act as porter; and the servant, stepping aside from the entrance, motioned the ladies to enter. They had no sooner done so than it shut, and excluded their guide. The two ladies found themselves in a small vestibule, illuminated by a dim lamp, and having, when the door was closed, no communication with the external light or air. The door of an inner apartment, partly open, was at the farther side of the vestibule.

'We must not hesitate now, Jemima,' said Lady Bothwell, and walked forwards into the inner room, where, surrounded by books, maps, philosophical utensils, and other implements of peculiar shape and appearance, they found the man of art.

There was nothing very peculiar in the Italian's appearance. He had the dark complexion and marked features of his country, seemed about fifty years old, and was handsomely but plainly dressed in a full suit of black clothes, which was then the universal costume of the medical profession. Large wax-lights, in silver sconces, illuminated the apartment, which was reasonably furnished. He rose as the ladies entered, and, notwithstanding the inferiority of their dress, received them with the marked respect due to their quality, and which foreigners are usually punctilious in rendering to those to whom such honours are due.

Lady Bothwell endeavoured to maintain her proposed incognito, and, as the Doctor ushered them to the upper end of the room, made a motion declining his courtesy, as unfitted for their condition. 'We are poor people, sir,' she said; 'only my sister's distress has brought us to consult your worship whether—'

He smiled as he interrupted her—'I am aware, madam, of your sister's distress, and its cause; I am aware, also, that I am honoured with a visit from two ladies of the highest consideration—Lady Bothwell and Lady Forester. If I could not distinguish them from the class of society which their present dress would indicate, there would be small possibility of my being able to gratify them by giving the information which they come to seek.'

'I can easily understand—' said Lady Bothwell.

'Pardon my boldness to interrupt you, milady,' cried the Italian; 'your ladyship was about to say that you could easily understand that I had got possession of your names by means of your domestic. But in thinking so, you do injustice to the fidelity of your servant, and, I may add, to the skill of one who is also not less your humble servant—Baptista Damiotti.'

'I have no intention to do either, sir,' said Lady Bothwell, maintaining a tone of composure, though somewhat surprised; 'but the situation is something new to me. If you know who we are, you also know, sir, what brought us here.'

'Curiosity to know the fate of a Scottish gentleman of rank, now, or lately, upon the Continent,' answered the seer. 'His name is Il Cavaliero Philippo Forester, a gentleman who has the honour to be husband to this lady, and, with your ladyship's permission for using plain language, the misfortune not to value as it deserves that inestimable advantage.'

Lady Forester sighed deeply, and Lady Bothwell replied,—

'Since you know our object without our telling it, the only question that remains is, whether you have the power to relieve my sister's anxiety?'

'I have, madam,' answered the Paduan scholar; 'but there is still a previous inquiry. Have you the courage to behold with your own eyes what the Cavaliero Philippo Forester is now doing? or will you take it on my report?'

'That question my sister must answer for herself,' said Lady Bothwell.

'With my own eyes will I endure to see whatever you have power to show me,' said Lady Forester, with the same determined spirit which had stimulated her since her resolution was taken upon this subject.

'There may be danger in it.'

'If gold can compensate the risk,' said Lady Forester, taking out her purse.

'I do not such things for the purpose of gain,' answered the foreigner; 'I dare not turn my art to such a purpose. If I take the gold of the wealthy, it is but to bestow it on the poor; nor do I ever accept more than the sum I have already received from your servant. Put up your purse, madam; an adept needs not your gold.'

Lady Bothwell, considering this rejection of her sister's offer as a mere trick of an empiric, to induce her to press a larger sum upon him, and willing that the scene should be commenced and ended, offered some gold in turn, observing that it was only to enlarge the sphere of his charity.

'Let Lady Bothwell enlarge the sphere of her own charity,' said the Paduan, 'not merely in giving of alms, in which I know she is not deficient, but in judging the character of others; and let her oblige Baptista Damiotti by believing him honest, till she shall discover him to be a knave. Do not be surprised, madam, if I speak in answer to your thoughts rather than your expressions; and tell me once more whether you have courage to look on what I am prepared to show?'

'I own, sir,' said Lady Bothwell, 'that your words strike me with some sense of fear; but whatever my sister desires to witness, I will not shrink from witnessing along with her.'

'Nay, the danger only consists in the risk of your resolution failing you. The sight can only last for the space of seven minutes; and should you interrupt the vision by speaking a single word, not only would the charm be broken, but some danger might result to the spectators. But if you can remain steadily silent for the seven minutes, your curiosity will be gratified without the slightest risk; and for this I will engage my honour.'

Internally Lady Bothwell thought the security was but an indifferent one; but she suppressed the suspicion, as if she had believed that the adept, whose dark features wore a half-formed smile, could in reality read even her most secret reflections. A solemn pause then ensued, until Lady Forester gathered courage enough to reply to the physician, as he termed himself, that she would abide with firmness and silence the sight which he had promised to exhibit to them. Upon this, he made them a low obeisance, and saying he went to prepare matters to meet their wish, left the apartment. The two sisters, hand in hand, as if seeking by that close union to divert any danger which might threaten them, sat down on two seats in immediate contact with each other—Jemima seeking support in the manly and habitual courage of Lady Bothwell; and she, on the other hand, more agitated than she had expected, endeavouring to fortify herself by the desperate resolution which circumstances had forced her sister to assume. The one perhaps said to herself that her sister never feared anything; and the other might reflect that what so feeble-minded a woman as Jemima did not fear, could not properly be a subject of apprehension to a person of firmness and resolution like her own.

In a few moments the thoughts of both were diverted from their own situation by a strain of music so singularly sweet and solemn that, while it seemed calculated to avert or dispel any feeling unconnected with its harmony, increased, at the same time, the solemn excitation which the preceding interview was calculated to produce. The music was that of some instrument with which they were unacquainted; but circumstances afterwards led my ancestress to believe that it was that of the harmonica, which she heard at a much later period in life.

When these heaven-born sounds had ceased, a door opened in the upper end of the apartment, and they saw Damiotti, standing at the head of two or three steps, sign to them to advance. His dress was so different from that which he had worn a few minutes before, that they could hardly recognize him; and the deadly paleness of his countenance, and a certain stern rigidity of muscles, like that of one whose mind is made up to some strange and daring action, had totally changed the somewhat sarcastic expression with which he had previously regarded them both, and particularly Lady Bothwell. He was barefooted, excepting a species of sandals in the antique fashion; his legs were naked beneath the knees; above them he wore hose, and a doublet of dark crimson silk close to his body; and over that a flowing loose robe, something resembling a surplice, of snow-white linen. His throat and neck were uncovered, and his long, straight, black hair was carefully combed down at full length.

As the ladies approached at his bidding, he showed no gesture of that ceremonious courtesy of which he had been formerly lavish. On the contrary, he made the signal of advance with an air of command; and when, arm in arm, and with insecure steps, the sisters approached the spot where he stood, it was with a warning frown that he pressed his finger to his lips, as if reiterating his condition of absolute silence, while, stalking before them, he led the way into the next apartment.

This was a large room, hung with black, as if for a funeral. At the upper end was a table, or rather a species of altar, covered with the same lugubrious colour, on which lay divers objects resembling the usual implements of sorcery. These objects were not indeed visible as they advanced into the apartment; for the light which displayed them, being only that of two expiring lamps, was extremely faint. The master—to use the Italian phrase for persons of this description—approached the upper end of the room, with a genuflection like that of a Catholic to the crucifix, and at the same time crossed himself. The ladies followed in silence, and arm in arm. Two or three low broad steps led to a platform in front of the altar, or what resembled such. Here the sage took his stand, and placed the ladies beside him, once more earnestly repeating by signs his injunctions of silence. The Italian then, extending his bare arm from under his linen vestment, pointed with his forefinger to five large flambeaux, or torches, placed on each side of the altar. They took fire successively at the approach of his hand, or rather of his finger, and spread a strong light through the room. By this the visitors could discern that, on the seeming altar, were disposed two naked swords laid crosswise; a large open book, which they conceived to be a copy of the Holy Scriptures, but in a language to them unknown; and beside this mysterious volume was placed a human skull. But what struck the sisters most was a very tall and broad mirror, which occupied all the space behind the altar, and, illumined by the lighted torches, reflected the mysterious articles which were laid upon it.

The master then placed himself between the two ladies, and, pointing to the mirror, took each by the hand, but without speaking a syllable. They gazed intently on the polished and sable space to which he had directed their attention. Suddenly the surface assumed a new and singular appearance. It no longer simply reflected the objects placed before it, but, as if it had self-contained scenery of its own, objects began to appear within it, at first in a disorderly, indistinct, and miscellaneous manner, like form arranging itself out of chaos; at length, in distinct and defined shape and symmetry. It was thus that, after some shifting of light and darkness over the face of the wonderful glass, a long perspective of arches and columns began to arrange itself on its sides, and a vaulted roof on the upper part of it, till, after many oscillations, the whole vision gained a fixed and stationary appearance, representing the interior of a foreign church. The pillars were stately, and hung with scutcheons; the arches were lofty and magnificent; the floor was lettered with funeral inscriptions. But there were no separate shrines, no images, no display of chalice or crucifix on the altar. It was, therefore, a Protestant church upon the Continent. A clergyman dressed in the Geneva gown and band stood by the communion table, and, with the Bible opened before him, and his clerk awaiting in the background, seemed prepared to perform some service of the church to which he belonged.

At length, there entered the middle aisle of the building a numerous party, which appeared to be a bridal one, as a lady and gentleman walked first, hand in hand, followed by a large concourse of persons of both sexes, gaily, nay richly, attired. The bride, whose features they could distinctly see, seemed not more than sixteen years old, and extremely beautiful. The bridegroom, for some seconds, moved rather with his shoulder towards them, and his face averted; but his elegance of form and step struck the sisters at once with the same apprehension. As he turned his face suddenly, it was frightfully realized, and they saw, in the gay bridegroom before them, Sir Philip Forester. His wife uttered an imperfect exclamation, at the sound of which the whole scene stirred and seemed to separate.

'I could compare it to nothing,' said Lady Bothwell, while recounting the wonderful tale, 'but to the dispersion of the reflection offered by a deep and calm pool, when a stone is suddenly cast into it, and the shadows become dissipated and broken.' The master pressed both the ladies' hands severely, as if to remind them of their promise, and of the danger which they incurred. The exclamation died away on Lady Forester's tongue, without attaining perfect utterance, and the scene in the glass, after the fluctuation of a minute, again resumed to the eye its former appearance of a real scene, existing within the mirror, as if represented in a picture, save that the figures were movable instead of being stationary.

The representation of Sir Philip Forester, now distinctly visible in form and feature, was seen to lead on towards the clergyman that beautiful girl, who advanced at once with diffidence and with a species of affectionate pride. In the meantime, and just as the clergyman had arranged the bridal company before him, and seemed about to commence the service, another group of persons, of whom two or three were officers, entered the church. They moved, at first, forward, as though they came to witness the bridal ceremony; but suddenly one of the officers, whose back was towards the spectators, detached himself from his companions, and rushed hastily towards the marriage party, when the whole of them turned towards him, as if attracted by some exclamation which had accompanied his advance. Suddenly the intruder drew his sword; the bridegroom unsheathed his own, and made towards him; swords were also drawn by other individuals, both of the marriage party and of those who had last entered. They fell into a sort of confusion, the clergyman, and some elder and graver persons, labouring apparently to keep the peace, while the hotter spirits on both sides brandished their weapons. But now, the period of the brief space during which the soothsayer, as he pretended, was permitted to exhibit his art, was arrived. The fumes again mixed together, and dissolved gradually from observation; the vaults and columns of the church rolled asunder, and disappeared; and the front of the mirror reflected nothing save the blazing torches and the melancholy apparatus placed on the altar or table before it.

The doctor led the ladies, who greatly required his support, into the apartment from whence they came, where wine, essences, and other means of restoring suspended animation, had been provided during his absence. He motioned them to chairs, which they occupied in silence—Lady Forester, in particular, wringing her hands, and casting her eyes up to heaven, but without speaking a word, as if the spell had been still before her eyes.

'And what we have seen is even now acting?' said Lady Bothwell, collecting herself with difficulty.

'That,' answered Baptista Damiotti, 'I cannot justly, or with certainty, say. But it is either now acting, or has been acted during a short space before this. It is the last remarkable transaction in which the Cavalier Forester has been engaged.'

Lady Bothwell then expressed anxiety concerning her sister, whose altered countenance and apparent unconsciousness of what passed around her excited her apprehensions how it might be possible to convey her home.

'I have prepared for that,' answered the adept. 'I have directed the servant to bring your equipage as near to this place as the narrowness of the street will permit. Fear not for your sister, but give her, when you return home, this composing draught, and she will be better to-morrow morning. Few,' he added in a melancholy tone, 'leave this house as well in health as they entered it. Such being the consequence of seeking knowledge by mysterious means, I leave you to judge the condition of those who have the power of gratifying such irregular curiosity. Farewell, and forget not the potion.'

'I will give her nothing that comes from you,' said Lady Bothwell; 'I have seen enough of your art already. Perhaps you would poison us both to conceal your own necromancy. But we are persons who want neither the means of making our wrongs known, nor the assistance of friends to right them.'

'You have had no wrongs from me, madam,' said the adept. 'You sought one who is little grateful for such honour. He seeks no one, and only gives responses to those who invite and call upon him. After all, you have but learned a little sooner the evil which you must still be doomed to endure. I hear your servant's step at the door, and will detain your ladyship and Lady Forester no longer. The next packet from the Continent will explain what you have already partly witnessed. Let it not, if I may advise, pass too suddenly into your sister's hands.'

So saying, he bid Lady Bothwell good-night. She went, lighted by the adept, to the vestibule, where he hastily threw a black cloak over his singular dress, and opening the door, entrusted his visitors to the care of the servant. It was with difficulty that Lady Bothwell sustained her sister to the carriage, though it was only twenty steps distant. When they arrived at home, Lady Forester required medical assistance. The physician of the family attended, and shook his head on feeling her pulse.

'Here has been,' he said, 'a violent and sudden shock on the nerves. I must know how it has happened.'

Lady Bothwell admitted they had visited the conjurer, and that Lady Forester had received some bad news respecting her husband, Sir Philip.

'That rascally quack would make my fortune, were he to stay in Edinburgh,' said the graduate; 'this is the seventh nervous case I have heard of his making for me, and all by effect of terror.' He next examined the composing draught which Lady Bothwell had unconsciously brought in her hand, tasted it, and pronounced it very germain to the matter, and what would save an application to the apothecary. He then paused, and looking at Lady Bothwell very significantly, at length added, 'I suppose I must not ask your ladyship anything about this Italian warlock's proceedings?'

'Indeed, doctor,' answered Lady Bothwell, 'I consider what passed as confidential; and though the man may be a rogue, yet, as we were fools enough to consult him, we should, I think, be honest enough to keep his counsel.'

'MAY be a knave! Come,' said the doctor, 'I am glad to hear your ladyship allows such a possibility in anything that comes from Italy.'

'What comes from Italy may be as good as what comes from Hanover, doctor. But you and I will remain good friends; and that it may be so, we will say nothing of Whig and Tory.'

'Not I,' said the doctor, receiving his fee, and taking his hat; 'a Carolus serves my purpose as well as a Willielmus. But I should like to know why old Lady Saint Ringan, and all that set, go about wasting their decayed lungs in puffing this foreign fellow.'

'Ay—you had best set him down a Jesuit, as Scrub says.' On these terms they parted.

The poor patient—whose nerves, from an extraordinary state of tension, had at length become relaxed in as extraordinary a degree—continued to struggle with a sort of imbecility, the growth of superstitious terror, when the shocking tidings were brought from Holland which fulfilled even her worst expectations.

They were sent by the celebrated Earl of Stair, and contained the melancholy event of a duel betwixt Sir Philip Forester and his wife's half-brother, Captain Falconer, of the Scotch-Dutch, as they were then called, in which the latter had been killed. The cause of quarrel rendered the incident still more shocking. It seemed that Sir Philip had left the army suddenly, in consequence of being unable to pay a very considerable sum which he had lost to another volunteer at play. He had changed his name, and taken up his residence at Rotterdam, where he had insinuated himself into the good graces of an ancient and rich burgomaster, and, by his handsome person and graceful manners, captivated the affections of his only child, a very young person, of great beauty, and the heiress of much wealth. Delighted with the specious attractions of his proposed son-in-law, the wealthy merchant—whose idea of the British character was too high to admit of his taking any precaution to acquire evidence of his condition and circumstances—gave his consent to the marriage. It was about to be celebrated in the principal church of the city, when it was interrupted by a singular occurrence.

Captain Falconer having been detached to Rotterdam to bring up a part of the brigade of Scottish auxiliaries, who were in quarters there, a person of consideration in the town, to whom he had been formerly known, proposed to him for amusement to go to the high church to see a countryman of his own married to the daughter of a wealthy burgomaster. Captain Falconer went accordingly, accompanied by his Dutch acquaintance, with a party of his friends, and two or three officers of the Scotch brigade. His astonishment may be conceived when he saw his own brother-in-law, a married man, on the point of leading to the altar the innocent and beautiful creature upon whom he was about to practise a base and unmanly deceit. He proclaimed his villainy on the spot, and the marriage was interrupted, of course. But against the opinion of more thinking men, who considered Sir Philip Forester as having thrown himself out of the rank of men of honour, Captain Falconer admitted him to the privilege of such, accepted a challenge from him, and in the rencounter received a mortal wound. Such are the ways of Heaven, mysterious in our eyes. Lady Forester never recovered the shock of this dismal intelligence.

'And did this tragedy,' said I, 'take place exactly at the time when the scene in the mirror was exhibited?'

'It is hard to be obliged to maim one's story,' answered my aunt, 'but to speak the truth, it happened some days sooner than the apparition was exhibited.'

'And so there remained a possibility,' said I, 'that by some secret and speedy communication the artist might have received early intelligence of that incident.'

'The incredulous pretended so,' replied my aunt.

'What became of the adept?' demanded I.

'Why, a warrant came down shortly afterwards to arrest him for high treason, as an agent of the Chevalier St. George; and Lady Bothwell, recollecting the hints which had escaped the doctor, an ardent friend of the Protestant succession, did then call to remembrance that this man was chiefly PRONE among the ancient matrons of her own political persuasion. It certainly seemed probable that intelligence from the Continent, which could easily have been transmitted by an active and powerful agent, might have enabled him to prepare such a scene of phantasmagoria as she had herself witnessed. Yet there were so many difficulties in assigning a natural explanation, that, to the day of her death, she remained in great doubt on the subject, and much disposed to cut the Gordian knot by admitting the existence of supernatural agency.'

'But, my dear aunt,' said I, 'what became of the man of skill?'

'Oh, he was too good a fortune-teller not to be able to foresee that his own destiny would be tragical if he waited the arrival of the man with the silver greyhound upon his sleeve. He made, as we say, a moonlight flitting, and was nowhere to be seen or heard of. Some noise there was about papers or letters found in the house; but it died away, and Doctor Baptista Damiotti was soon as little talked of as Galen or Hippocrates.'

'And Sir Philip Forester,' said I, 'did he too vanish for ever from the public scene?'

'No,' replied my kind informer. 'He was heard of once more, and it was upon a remarkable occasion. It is said that we Scots, when there was such a nation in existence, have, among our full peck of virtues, one or two little barley-corns of vice. In particular, it is alleged that we rarely forgive, and never forget, any injuries received—that we make an idol of our resentment, as poor Lady Constance did of her grief, and are addicted, as Burns says, to "nursing our wrath to keep it warm." Lady Bothwell was not without this feeling; and, I believe, nothing whatever, scarce the restoration of the Stewart line, could have happened so delicious to her feelings as an opportunity of being revenged on Sir Philip Forester for the deep and double injury which had deprived her of a sister and of a brother. But nothing of him was heard or known till many a year had passed away.

'At length—it was on a Fastern's E'en (Shrovetide) assembly, at which the whole fashion of Edinburgh attended, full and frequent, and when Lady Bothwell had a seat amongst the lady patronesses, that one of the attendants on the company whispered into her ear that a gentleman wished to speak with her in private.

'"In private? and in an assembly room?—he must be mad. Tell him to call upon me to-morrow morning."

'"I said so, my lady," answered the man, "but he desired me to give you this paper."

'She undid the billet, which was curiously folded and sealed. It only bore the words, "ON BUSINESS OF LIFE AND DEATH," written in a hand which she had never seen before. Suddenly it occurred to her that it might concern the safety of some of her political friends. She therefore followed the messenger to a small apartment where the refreshments were prepared, and from which the general company was excluded. She found an old man, who, at her approach, rose up and bowed profoundly. His appearance indicated a broken constitution, and his dress, though sedulously rendered conforming to the etiquette of a ballroom, was worn and tarnished, and hung in folds about his emaciated person. Lady Bothwell was about to feel for her purse, expecting to get rid of the supplicant at the expense of a little money, but some fear of a mistake arrested her purpose. She therefore gave the man leisure to explain himself.

"'I have the honour to speak with the Lady Bothwell?'"

"'I am Lady Bothwell; allow me to say that this is no time or place for long explanations. What are your commands with me?'"

"'Your ladyship,' said the old man, 'had once a sister.'"

"'True; whom I loved as my own soul.'"

"'And a brother.'"

"'The bravest, the kindest, the most affectionate!'" said Lady Bothwell.

"'Both these beloved relatives you lost by the fault of an unfortunate man,'" continued the stranger.

"'By the crime of an unnatural, bloody-minded murderer,'" said the lady.

"'I am answered,' replied the old man, bowing, as if to withdraw.

"'Stop, sir, I command you,'" said Lady Bothwell. "Who are you that, at such a place and time, come to recall these horrible recollections? I insist upon knowing.'"

"'I am one who intends Lady Bothwell no injury, but, on the contrary, to offer her the means of doing a deed of Christian charity, which the world would wonder at, and which Heaven would reward; but I find her in no temper for such a sacrifice as I was prepared to ask."

"'Speak out, sir; what is your meaning?" said Lady Bothwell.

"'The wretch that has wronged you so deeply," rejoined the stranger, "is now on his death-bed. His days have been days of misery, his nights have been sleepless hours of anguish—yet he cannot die without your forgiveness. His life has been an unremitting penance—yet he dares not part from his burden while your curses load his soul."

"'Tell him," said Lady Bothwell sternly, "to ask pardon of that Being whom he has so greatly offended, not of an erring mortal like himself. What could my forgiveness avail him?"

"'Much," answered the old man. "It will be an earnest of that which he may then venture to ask from his Creator, lady, and from yours. Remember, Lady Bothwell, you too have a death-bed to look forward to; Your soul may—all human souls must—feel the awe of facing the judgment-seat, with the wounds of an untented conscience, raw, and rankling—what thought would it be then that should whisper, 'I have given no mercy, how then shall I ask it?'"

"'Man, whosoever thou mayest be," replied Lady Bothwell, "urge me not so cruelly. It would be but blasphemous hypocrisy to utter with my lips the words which every throb of my heart protests against. They would open the earth and give to light the wasted form of my sister, the bloody form of my murdered brother. Forgive him?—never, never!"

"'Great God!" cried the old man, holding up his hands, "is it thus the worms which Thou hast called out of dust obey the commands of their Maker? Farewell, proud and unforgiving woman. Exult that thou hast added to a death in want and pain the agonies of religious despair; but never again mock Heaven by petitioning for the pardon which thou hast refused to grant."

'He was turning from her.

"'Stop,'" she exclaimed; "I will try—yes, I will try to pardon him."

"'Gracious lady,'" said the old man, "you will relieve the over-burdened soul which dare not sever itself from its sinful companion of earth without being at peace with you. What do I know—your forgiveness may perhaps preserve for penitence the dregs of a wretched life."

"'Ha!' said the lady, as a sudden light broke on her, 'it is the villain himself!'" And grasping Sir Philip Forester—for it was he, and no other—by the collar, she raised a cry of "Murder, murder! seize the murderer!"

'At an exclamation so singular, in such a place, the company thronged into the apartment; but Sir Philip Forester was no longer there. He had forcibly extricated himself from Lady Bothwell's hold, and had run out of the apartment, which opened on the landing-place of the stair. There seemed no escape in that direction, for there were several persons coming up the steps, and others descending. But the unfortunate man was desperate. He threw himself over the balustrade, and alighted safely in the lobby, though a leap of fifteen feet at least, then dashed into the street, and was lost in darkness. Some of the Bothwell family made pursuit, and had they come up with the fugitive they might perhaps have slain him; for in those days men's blood ran warm in their veins. But the police did not interfere, the matter most criminal having happened long since, and in a foreign land. Indeed it was always thought that this extraordinary scene originated in a hypocritical experiment, by which Sir Philip desired to ascertain whether he might return to his native country in safety from the resentment of a family which he had injured so deeply. As the result fell out so contrary to his wishes, he is believed to have returned to the Continent, and there died in exile.'

So closed the tale of the MYSTERIOUS MIRROR.

2

THE TAPESTRIED CHAMBER

The following narrative is given from the pen, so far as memory permits, in the same character in which it was presented to the author's ear; nor has he claim to further praise, or to be more deeply censured, than in proportion to the good or bad judgment which he has employed in selecting his materials, as he has studiously avoided any attempt at ornament which might interfere with the simplicity of the tale.

At the same time, it must be admitted that the particular class of stories which turns on the marvellous possesses a stronger influence when told than when committed to print. The volume taken up at noonday, though rehearsing the same incidents, conveys a much more feeble impression than is achieved by the voice of the speaker on a circle of fireside auditors, who hang upon the narrative as the narrator details the minute incidents which serve to give it authenticity, and lowers his voice with an affectation of mystery while he approaches the fearful and wonderful part. It was with such advantages that the present writer heard the following events related, more than twenty years since, by the celebrated Miss Seward of Litchfield, who, to her numerous accomplishments, added, in a remarkable degree, the power of narrative in private conversation. In its present form the tale must necessarily lose all the interest which was attached to it by the flexible voice and intelligent features of the gifted narrator. Yet still, read aloud to an undoubting audience by the doubtful light of the closing evening, or in silence by a decaying taper, and amidst the solitude of a half-lighted apartment, it may redeem its character as a good ghost story. Miss Seward always affirmed that she had derived her information from an authentic source, although she suppressed the names of the two persons chiefly concerned. I will not avail myself of any particulars I may have since received concerning the localities of the detail, but suffer them to rest under the same general description in which they were first related to me; and for the same reason I will not add to or diminish the narrative by any circumstance, whether more or less material, but simply rehearse, as I heard it, a story of supernatural terror.

About the end of the American war, when the officers of Lord Cornwallis's army, which surrendered at Yorktown, and others, who had been made prisoners during the impolitic and ill-fated controversy, were returning to their own country, to relate their adventures, and repose themselves after their fatigues, there was amongst them a general officer, to whom Miss S. gave the name of Browne, but merely, as I understood, to save the inconvenience of introducing a nameless agent in the narrative. He was an officer of merit, as well as a gentleman of high consideration for family and attainments.

Some business had carried General Browne upon a tour through the western counties, when, in the conclusion of a morning stage, he found himself in the vicinity of a small country town, which presented a scene of uncommon beauty, and of a character peculiarly English.

The little town, with its stately old church, whose tower bore testimony to the devotion of ages long past, lay amidst pastures and cornfields of small extent, but bounded and divided with hedgerow timber of great age and size. There were few marks of modern improvement. The environs of the place intimated neither the solitude of decay nor the bustle of novelty; the houses were old, but in good repair; and the beautiful little river murmured freely on its way to the left of the town, neither restrained by a dam nor bordered by a towing-path.

Upon a gentle eminence, nearly a mile to the southward of the town, were seen, amongst many venerable oaks and tangled thickets, the turrets of a castle as old as the walls of York and Lancaster, but which seemed to have received important alterations during the age of Elizabeth and her successor. It had not been a place of great size; but whatever accommodation it formerly afforded was, it must be supposed, still to be obtained within its walls. At least, such was the inference which General Browne drew from observing the smoke arise merrily from several of the ancient wreathed and carved chimney-stalks. The wall of the park ran alongside of the highway for two or three hundred yards; and through the different points by which the eye found glimpses into the woodland scenery, it seemed to be well stocked. Other points of view opened in succession—now a full one of the front of the old castle, and now a side glimpse at its particular towers, the former rich in all the bizarrerie of the Elizabethan school, while the simple and solid strength of other parts of the building seemed to show that they had been raised more for defence than ostentation.

Delighted with the partial glimpses which he obtained of the castle through the woods and glades by which this ancient feudal fortress was surrounded, our military traveller was determined to inquire whether it might not deserve a nearer view, and whether it contained family pictures or other objects of curiosity worthy of a stranger's visit, when, leaving the vicinity of the park, he rolled through a clean and well-paved street, and stopped at the door of a well-frequented inn.

Before ordering horses, to proceed on his journey, General Browne made inquiries concerning the proprietor of the chateau which had so attracted his admiration, and was equally surprised and pleased at hearing in reply a nobleman named, whom we shall call Lord Woodville. How fortunate! Much of Browne's early recollections, both at school and at college, had been connected with young Woodville, whom, by a few questions, he now ascertained to be the same with the owner of this fair domain. He had been raised to the peerage by the decease of his father a few months before, and, as the General learned from the landlord, the term of mourning being ended, was now taking possession of his paternal estate in the jovial season of merry, autumn, accompanied by a select party of friends, to enjoy the sports of a country famous for game.

This was delightful news to our traveller. Frank Woodville had been Richard Browne's fag at Eton, and his chosen intimate at Christ Church; their pleasures and their tasks had been the same; and the honest soldier's heart warmed to find his early friend in possession of so delightful a residence, and of an estate, as the landlord assured him with a nod and a wink, fully adequate to maintain and add to his dignity. Nothing was more natural than that the traveller should suspend a journey, which there was nothing to render hurried, to pay a visit to an old friend under such agreeable circumstances.

The fresh horses, therefore, had only the brief task of conveying the General's travelling carriage to Woodville Castle. A porter admitted them at a modern Gothic lodge, built in that style to correspond with the castle itself, and at the same time rang a bell to give warning of the approach of visitors. Apparently the sound of the bell had suspended the separation of the company, bent on the various amusements of the morning; for, on entering the court of the chateau, several young men were lounging about in their sporting dresses, looking at and criticizing the dogs which the keepers held in readiness to attend their pastime. As General Browne alighted, the young lord came to the gate of the hall, and for an instant gazed, as at a stranger, upon the countenance of his friend, on which war, with its fatigues and its wounds, had made a great alteration. But the uncertainty lasted no longer than till the visitor had spoken, and the hearty greeting which followed was such as can only be exchanged betwixt those who have passed together the merry days of careless boyhood or early youth.

'If I could have formed a wish, my dear Browne,' said Lord Woodville, 'it would have been to have you here, of all men, upon this occasion, which my friends are good enough to hold as a sort of holiday. Do not think you have been unwatched during the years you have been absent from us. I have traced you through your dangers, your triumphs, your misfortunes, and was delighted to see that, whether in victory or defeat, the name of my old friend was always distinguished with applause.'

The General made a suitable reply, and congratulated his friend on his new dignities, and the possession of a place and domain so beautiful.

'Nay, you have seen nothing of it as yet,' said Lord Woodville, 'and I trust you do not mean to leave us till you are better acquainted with it. It is true, I confess, that my present party is pretty large, and the old house, like other places of the kind, does not possess so much accommodation as the extent of the outward walls appears to promise. But we can give you a comfortable old-fashioned room, and I venture to suppose that your campaigns have taught you to be glad of worse quarters.'

The General shrugged his shoulders, and laughed. 'I presume,' he said, 'the worst apartment in your chateau is considerably superior to the old tobacco-cask in which I was fain to take up my night's lodging when I was in the Bush, as the Virginians call it, with the light corps. There I lay, like Diogenes himself, so delighted with my covering from the elements, that I made a vain attempt to have it rolled on to my next quarters; but my commander for the time would give way to no such luxurious provision, and I took farewell of my beloved cask with tears in my eyes.'

'Well, then, since you do not fear your quarters,' said Lord Woodville, 'you will stay with me a week at least. Of guns, dogs, fishing-rods, flies, and means of sport by sea and land, we have enough and to spare—you cannot pitch on an amusement but we will find the means of pursuing it. But if you prefer the gun and pointers, I will go with you myself, and see whether you have mended your shooting since you have been amongst the Indians of the back settlements.'

The General gladly accepted his friendly host's proposal in all its points. After a morning of manly exercise, the company met at dinner, where it was the delight of Lord Woodville to conduce to the display of the high properties of his recovered friend, so as to recommend him to his guests, most of whom were persons of distinction. He led General Browne to speak of the scenes he had witnessed; and as every word marked alike the brave officer and the sensible man, who retained possession of his cool judgment under the most imminent dangers, the company looked upon the soldier with general respect, as on one who had proved himself possessed of an uncommon portion of personal courage—that attribute of all others of which everybody desires to be thought possessed.

The day at Woodville Castle ended as usual in such mansions. The hospitality stopped within the limits of good order. Music, in which the young lord was a proficient, succeeded to the circulation of the bottle; cards and billiards, for those who preferred such amusements, were in readiness; but the exercise of the morning required early hours, and not long after eleven o'clock the guests began to retire to their several apartments.

The young lord himself conducted his friend, General Browne, to the chamber destined for him, which answered the description he had given of it, being comfortable, but old-fashioned. The bed was of the massive form used in the end of the seventeenth century, and the curtains of faded silk, heavily trimmed with tarnished gold. But then the sheets, pillows, and blankets looked delightful to the campaigner, when he thought of his 'mansion, the cask.' There was an air of gloom in the tapestry hangings, which, with their worn-out graces, curtained the walls of the little chamber, and gently undulated as the autumnal breeze found its way through the ancient lattice window, which pattered and whistled as the air gained entrance. The toilet, too, with its mirror, turbaned after the manner of the beginning of the century, with a coiffure of murrey-coloured silk, and its hundred strange-shaped boxes, providing for arrangements which had been obsolete for more than fifty years, had an antique, and in so far a melancholy, aspect. But nothing could blaze more brightly and cheerfully than the two large wax candles; or if aught could rival them, it was the flaming, bickering fagots in the chimney, that sent at once their gleam and their warmth through the snug apartment, which, notwithstanding the general antiquity of its appearance, was not wanting in the least convenience that modern habits rendered either necessary or desirable.

'This is an old-fashioned sleeping apartment, General,' said the young lord; 'but I hope you find nothing that makes you envy your old tobacco-cask.'

'I am not particular respecting my lodgings,' replied the General; 'yet were I to make any choice, I would prefer this chamber by many degrees to the gayer and more modern rooms of your family mansion. Believe me that, when I unite its modern air of comfort with its venerable antiquity, and recollect that it is your lordship's property, I shall feel in better quarters here than if I were in the best hotel London could afford.'

'I trust—I have no doubt—that you will find yourself as comfortable as I wish you, my dear General,' said the young nobleman; and once more bidding his guest good-night, he shook him by the hand, and withdrew.

The General once more looked round him, and internally congratulating himself on his return to peaceful life, the comforts of which were endeared by the recollection of the hardships and dangers he had lately sustained, undressed himself, and prepared for a luxurious night's rest.

Here, contrary to the custom of this species of tale, we leave the General in possession of his apartment until the next morning.

The company assembled for breakfast at an early hour, but without the appearance of General Browne, who seemed the guest that Lord Woodville was desirous of honouring above all whom his hospitality had assembled around him. He more than once expressed surprise at the General's absence, and at length sent a servant to make inquiry after him. The man brought back information that General Browne had been walking abroad since an early hour of the morning, in defiance of the weather, which was misty and ungenial.

'The custom of a soldier,' said the young nobleman to his friends. 'Many of them acquire habitual vigilance, and cannot sleep after the early hour at which their duty usually commands them to be alert.'

Yet the explanation which Lord Woodville thus offered to the company seemed hardly satisfactory to his own mind, and it was in a fit of silence and abstraction that he waited the return of the General. It took place near an hour after the breakfast bell had rung. He looked fatigued and feverish. His hair, the powdering and arrangement of which was at this time one of the most important occupations of a man's whole day, and marked his fashion as much as in the present time the tying of a cravat, or the want of one, was dishevelled, uncurled, void of powder, and dank with dew. His clothes were huddled on with a careless negligence, remarkable in a military man, whose real or supposed duties are usually held to include some attention to the toilet; and his looks were haggard and ghastly in a peculiar degree.

'So you have stolen a march upon us this morning, my dear General,' said Lord Woodville; 'or you have not found your bed so much to your mind as I had hoped and you seemed to expect. How did you rest last night?'

'Oh, excellently well! remarkably well! never better in my life,' said General Browne rapidly, and yet with an air of embarrassment which was obvious to his friend. He then hastily swallowed a cup of tea, and neglecting or refusing whatever else was offered, seemed to fall into a fit of abstraction.

'You will take the gun to-day, General?' said his friend and host, but had to repeat the question twice ere he received the abrupt answer, 'No, my lord; I am sorry I cannot have the opportunity of spending another day with your lordship; my post horses are ordered, and will be here directly.'

All who were present showed surprise, and Lord Woodville immediately replied 'Post horses, my good friend! What can you possibly want with them when you promised to stay with me quietly for at least a week?'

'I believe,' said the General, obviously much embarrassed, 'that I might, in the pleasure of my first meeting with your lordship, have said something about stopping here a few days; but I have since found it altogether impossible.'

'That is very extraordinary,' answered the young nobleman. 'You seemed quite disengaged yesterday, and you cannot have had a summons to-day, for our post has not come up from the town, and therefore you cannot have received any letters.'

General Browne, without giving any further explanation, muttered something about indispensable business, and insisted on the absolute necessity of his departure in a manner which silenced all opposition on the part of his host, who saw that his resolution was taken, and forbore all further importunity.

'At least, however,' he said, 'permit me, my dear Browne, since go you will or must, to show you the view from the terrace, which the mist, that is now rising, will soon display.'

He threw open a sash-window, and stepped down upon the terrace as he spoke. The General followed him mechanically, but seemed little to attend to what his host was saying, as, looking across an extended and rich prospect, he pointed out the different objects worthy of observation. Thus they moved on till Lord Woodville had attained his purpose of drawing his guest entirely apart from the rest of the company, when, turning round upon him with an air of great solemnity, he addressed him thus:—

'Richard Browne, my old and very dear friend, we are now alone. Let me conjure you to answer me upon the word of a friend, and the honour of a soldier. How did you in reality rest during last night?'

'Most wretchedly indeed, my lord,' answered the General, in the same tone of solemnity—'so miserably, that I would not run the risk of such a second night, not only for all the lands belonging to this castle, but for all the country which I see from this elevated point of view.'

'This is most extraordinary,' said the young lord, as if speaking to himself; 'then there must be something in the reports concerning that apartment.' Again turning to the General, he said, 'For God's sake, my dear friend, be candid with me, and let me know the disagreeable particulars which have befallen you under a roof, where, with consent of the owner, you should have met nothing save comfort.'

The General seemed distressed by this appeal, and paused a moment before he replied. 'My dear lord,' he at length said, 'what happened to me last night is of a nature so peculiar and so unpleasant, that I could hardly bring myself to detail it even to your lordship, were it not that, independent of my wish to gratify any request of yours, I think that sincerity on my part may lead to some explanation about a circumstance equally painful and mysterious. To others, the communication I am about to make, might place me in the light of a weak-minded, superstitious fool, who suffered his own imagination to delude and bewilder him; but you have known me in childhood and youth, and will not suspect me of having adopted in manhood the feelings and frailties from which my early years were free.' Here he paused, and his friend replied,—

'Do not doubt my perfect confidence in the truth of your communication, however strange it may be,' replied Lord Woodville. 'I know your firmness of disposition too well, to suspect you could be made the object of imposition, and am aware that your honour and your friendship will equally deter you from exaggerating whatever you may have witnessed.'

'Well, then,' said the General, 'I will proceed with my story as well as I can, relying upon your candour, and yet distinctly feeling that I would rather face a battery than recall to my mind the odious recollections of last night.'

He paused a second time, and then perceiving that Lord Woodville remained silent and in an attitude of attention, he commenced, though not without obvious reluctance, the history of his night's adventures in the Tapestried Chamber.

'I undressed and went to bed so soon as your lordship left me yesterday evening; but the wood in the chimney, which nearly fronted my bed, blazed brightly and cheerfully, and, aided by a hundred exciting recollections of my childhood and youth, which had been recalled by the unexpected pleasure of meeting your lordship, prevented me from falling immediately asleep. I ought, however, to say that these reflections were all of a pleasant and agreeable kind, grounded on a sense of having for a time exchanged the labour, fatigues, and dangers of my profession for the enjoyments of a peaceful life, and the reunion of those friendly and affectionate ties which I had torn asunder at the rude summons of war.

'While such pleasing reflections were stealing over my mind, and gradually lulling me to slumber, I was suddenly aroused by a sound like that of the rustling of a silken gown, and the tapping of a pair of high-heeled shoes, as if a woman were walking in the apartment. Ere I could draw the curtain to see what the matter was, the figure of a little woman passed between the bed and the fire. The back of this form was turned to me, and I could observe, from the shoulders and neck, it was that of an old woman, whose dress was an old-fashioned gown, which I think ladies call a sacque—that is, a sort of robe completely loose in the body, but gathered into broad plaits upon the neck and shoulders, which fall down to the ground, and terminate in a species of train.

'I thought the intrusion singular enough, but never harboured for a moment the idea that what I saw was anything more than the mortal form of some old woman about the establishment, who had a fancy to dress like her grandmother, and who, having perhaps (as your lordship mentioned that you were rather straitened for room) been dislodged from her chamber for my accommodation, had forgotten the circumstance, and returned by twelve to her old haunt. Under this persuasion I moved myself in bed and coughed a little, to make the intruder sensible of my being in possession of the premises. She turned slowly round, but, gracious Heaven! my lord, what a countenance did she display to me! There was no longer any question what she was, or any thought of her being a living being. Upon a face which wore the fixed features of a corpse were imprinted the traces of the vilest and most hideous passions which had animated her while she lived. The body of some atrocious criminal seemed to have been given up from the grave, and the soul restored from the penal fire, in order to form for a space a union with the ancient accomplice of its guilt. I started up in bed, and sat upright, supporting myself on my palms, as I gazed on this horrible spectre. The hag made, as it seemed, a single and swift stride to the bed where I lay, and squatted herself down upon it, in precisely the same attitude which I had assumed in the extremity of horror, advancing her diabolical countenance within half a yard of mine, with a grin which seemed to intimate the malice and the derision of an incarnate fiend.'

Here General Browne stopped, and wiped from his brow the cold perspiration with which the recollection of his horrible vision had covered it.

'My lord,' he said, 'I am no coward, I have been in all the mortal dangers incidental to my profession, and I may truly boast that no man ever knew Richard Browne dishonour the sword he wears; but in these horrible circumstances, under the eyes, and, as it seemed, almost in the grasp of an incarnation of an evil spirit, all firmness forsook me, all manhood melted from me like wax in the furnace, and I felt my hair individually bristle. The current of my life-blood ceased to flow, and I sank back in a swoon, as very a victim to panic terror as ever was a village girl, or a child of ten years old. How long I lay in this condition I cannot pretend to guess.

'But I was roused by the castle clock striking one, so loud that it seemed as if it were in the very room. It was some time before I dared open my eyes, lest they should again encounter the horrible spectacle. When, however, I summoned courage to look up, she was no longer visible. My first idea was to pull my bell, wake the servants, and remove to a garret or a hay-loft, to be ensured against a second visitation. Nay, I will confess the truth that my resolution was altered, not by the shame of exposing myself, but by the fear that, as the bell-cord hung by the chimney, I might, in making my way to it, be again crossed by the fiendish hag, who, I figured to myself, might be still lurking about some corner of the apartment.

'I will not pretend to describe what hot and cold fever-fits tormented me for the rest of the night, through broken sleep, weary vigils, and that dubious state which forms the neutral ground between them. A hundred terrible objects appeared to haunt me; but there was the great difference betwixt the vision which I have described, and those which followed, that I knew the last to be deceptions of my own fancy and over-excited nerves.

'Day at last appeared, and I rose from my bed ill in health and humiliated in mind. I was ashamed of myself as a man and a soldier, and still more so at feeling my own extreme desire to escape from the haunted apartment, which, however, conquered all other considerations; so that, huddling on my clothes with the most careless haste, I made my escape from your lordship's mansion, to seek in the open air some relief to my nervous system, shaken as it was by this horrible rencounter with a visitant, for such I must believe her, from the other world. Your lordship has now heard the cause of my discomposure, and of my sudden desire to leave your hospitable castle. In other places I trust we may often meet, but God protect me from ever spending a second night under that roof!'

Strange as the General's tale was, he spoke with such a deep air of conviction that it cut short all the usual commentaries which are made on such stories. Lord Woodville never once asked him if he was sure he did not dream of the apparition, or suggested any of the possibilities by which it is fashionable to explain supernatural appearances as wild vagaries of the fancy, or deceptions of the optic nerves. On the contrary, he seemed deeply impressed with the truth and reality of what he had heard; and, after a considerable pause regretted, with much appearance of sincerity, that his early friend should in his house have suffered so severely.

'I am the more sorry for your pain, my dear Browne,' he continued, 'that it is the unhappy, though most unexpected, result of an experiment of my own. You must know that, for my father and grandfather's time, at least, the apartment which was assigned to you last night had been shut on account of reports that it was disturbed by supernatural sights and noises. When I came, a few weeks since, into possession of the estate, I thought the accommodation which the castle afforded for my friends was not extensive enough to permit the inhabitants of the invisible world to retain possession of a comfortable sleeping apartment. I therefore caused the Tapestried Chamber, as we call it, to be opened, and, without destroying its air of antiquity, I had such new articles of furniture placed in it as became the modern times. Yet, as the opinion that the room was haunted very strongly prevailed among the domestics, and was also known in the neighbourhood and to many of my friends, I feared some prejudice might be entertained by the first occupant of the Tapestried Chamber, which might tend to revive the evil report which it had laboured under, and so disappoint my purpose of rendering it a useful part or the house. I must confess, my dear Browne, that your arrival yesterday, agreeable to me for a thousand reasons besides, seemed the most favourable opportunity of removing the unpleasant rumours which attached to the room, since your courage was indubitable, and your mind free of any preoccupation on the subject. I could not, therefore, have chosen a more fitting subject for my experiment.'

'Upon my life,' said General Browne, somewhat hastily, 'I am infinitely obliged to your lordship—very particularly indebted indeed. I am likely to remember for some time the consequences of the experiment, as your lordship is pleased to call it.'

'Nay, now you are unjust, my dear friend,' said Lord Woodville. 'You have only to reflect for a single moment, in order to be convinced that I could not augur the possibility of the pain to which you have been so unhappily exposed. I was yesterday morning a complete sceptic on the subject of supernatural appearances. Nay, I am sure that, had I told you what was said about that room, those very reports would have induced you, by your own choice, to select it for your accommodation. It was my misfortune, perhaps my error, but really cannot be termed my fault, that you have been afflicted so strangely.'

'Strangely indeed!' said the General, resuming his good temper; 'and I acknowledge that I have no right to be offended with your lordship for treating me like what I used to think myself—a man of some firmness and courage. But I see my post horses are arrived, and I must not detain your lordship from your amusement.'

'Nay, my old friend,' said Lord Woodville, 'since you cannot stay with us another day—which, indeed, I can no longer urge—give me at least half an hour more. You used to love pictures, and I have a gallery of portraits, some of them by Vandyke, representing ancestry to whom this property and castle formerly belonged. I think that several of them will strike you as possessing merit.'

General Browne accepted the invitation, though somewhat unwillingly. It was evident he was not to breathe freely or at ease till he left Woodville Castle far behind him. He could not refuse his friend's invitation, however; and the less so, that he was a little ashamed of the peevishness which he had displayed towards his well-meaning entertainer.

The General, therefore, followed Lord Woodville through several rooms into a long gallery hung with pictures, which the latter pointed out to his guest, telling the names, and giving some account of the personages whose portraits presented themselves in progression. General Browne was but little interested in the details which these accounts conveyed to him. They were, indeed, of the kind which are usually found in an old family gallery. Here was a Cavalier who had ruined the estate in the royal cause; there a fine lady who had reinstated it by contracting a match with a wealthy Roundhead. There hung a gallant who had been in danger for corresponding with the exiled Court at Saint Germain's; here one who had taken arms for William at the Revolution; and there a third that had thrown his weight alternately into the scale of Whig and Tory.

While Lord Woodville was cramming these words into his guest's ear, 'against the stomach of his sense,' they gained the middle of the gallery, when he beheld General Browne suddenly start, and assume an attitude of the utmost surprise, not unmixed with fear, as his eyes were suddenly caught and riveted by a portrait of an old lady in a sacque, the fashionable dress of the end of the seventeenth century.

'There she is!' he exclaimed—'there she is, in form and features, though Inferior in demoniac expression to the accursed hag who visited me last night!'

'If that be the case,' said the young nobleman, 'there can remain no longer any doubt of the horrible reality of your apparition. That is the picture of a wretched ancestress of mine, of whose crimes a black and fearful catalogue is recorded in a family history in my charter-chest. The recital of them would be too horrible; it is enough to say, that in yon fatal apartment incest and unnatural murder were committed. I will restore it to the solitude to which the better judgment of those who preceded me had consigned it; and never shall any one, so long as I can prevent it, be exposed to a repetition of the supernatural horrors which could shake such courage as yours.'

Thus the friends, who had met with such glee, parted in a very different mood—Lord Woodville to command the Tapestried Chamber to be unmantled, and the door built up; and General Browne to seek in some less beautiful country, and with some less dignified friend, forgetfulness of the painful night which he had passed in Woodville Castle.

3

DEATH OF THE LAIRD'S JOCK

[The manner in which this trifle was introduced at the time to Mr F. M. Reynolds, editor of The Keepsake of 1828, leaves no occasion for a preface.]

AUGUST 1831.

TO THE EDITOR OF THE KEEPSAKE.

You have asked me, sir, to point out a subject for the pencil, and I feel the difficulty of complying with your request, although I am not certainly unaccustomed to literary composition, or a total stranger to the stores of history and tradition, which afford the best copies for the painter's art. But although SICUT PICTURA POESIS is an ancient and undisputed axiom—although poetry and painting both address themselves to the same object of exciting the human imagination, by presenting to it pleasing or sublime images of ideal scenes—yet the one conveying itself through the ears to the understanding, and the other applying itself only to the eyes, the subjects which are best suited to the bard or tale-teller are often totally unfit for painting, where the artist must present in a single glance all that his art has power to tell us. The artist can neither recapitulate the past nor intimate the future. The single NOW is all which he can present; and hence, unquestionably, many subjects which delight us in poetry or in narrative, whether real or fictitious, cannot with advantage be transferred to the canvas.

Being in some degree aware of these difficulties, though doubtless unacquainted both with their extent and the means by which they may be modified or surmounted, I have, nevertheless, ventured to draw up the following traditional narrative as a story in which, when the general details are known, the interest is so much concentrated in one strong moment of agonizing passion, that it can be understood and sympathized with at a single glance. I therefore presume that it may be acceptable as a hint to some one among the numerous artists who have of late years distinguished themselves as rearing up and supporting the British school.

Enough has been said and sung about
'The well-contested ground, The warlike Border-land,'
to render the habits of the tribes who inhabited it before the union of England and Scotland familiar to most of your readers. The rougher and sterner features of their character were softened by their attachment to the fine arts, from which has arisen the saying that on the frontiers every dale had its battle, and every river its song. A rude species of chivalry was in constant use, and single combats were practised as the amusement of the few intervals of truce which suspended the exercise of war. The inveteracy of this custom may be inferred from the following incident:—

Bernard Gilpin, the apostle of the north, the first who undertook to preach the Protestant doctrines to the Border dalesmen, was surprised, on entering one of their churches, to see a gauntlet or mail-glove hanging above the altar. Upon inquiring; the meaning of a symbol so indecorous being displayed in that sacred place, he was informed by the clerk that the glove was that of a famous swordsman, who hung it there as an emblem of a general challenge and gage of battle to any who should dare to take the fatal token down. 'Reach it to me,' said the reverend churchman. The clerk and the sexton equally declined the perilous office, and the good Bernard Gilpin was obliged to remove the glove with his own hands, desiring those who were present to inform the champion that he, and no other, had possessed himself of the gage of defiance. But the champion was as much ashamed to face Bernard Gilpin as the officials of the church had been to displace his pledge of combat.

The date of the following story is about the latter years of Queen Elizabeth's reign; and the events took place in Liddesdale, a hilly and pastoral district of Roxburghshire, which, on a part of its boundary, is divided from England only by a small river.

During the good old times of RUGGING AND RIVING—that is, tugging and tearing—under which term the disorderly doings of the warlike age are affectionately remembered, this valley was principally cultivated by the sept or clan of the Armstrongs. The chief of this warlike race was the Laird of Mangerton. At the period of which I speak, the estate of Mangerton, with the power and dignity of chief, was possessed by John Armstrong, a man of great size, strength, and courage. While his father was alive, he was distinguished from others of his clan who bore the same name, by the epithet of the LAIRD'S JOCK—that is to say, the Laird's son Jock, or Jack. This name he distinguished by so many bold and desperate achievements, that he retained it even after his father's death, and is mentioned under it both in authentic records and in tradition. Some of his feats are recorded in the minstrelsy of the Scottish Border, and others are mentioned in contemporary chronicles.

At the species of singular combat which we have described the Laird's Jock was unrivalled, and no champion of Cumberland, Westmoreland, or Northumberland could endure the sway of the huge two-handed sword which he wielded, and which few others could even lift. This 'awful sword,' as the common people term it, was as dear to him as Durindana or Fushberta to their respective masters, and was nearly as formidable to his enemies as those renowned falchions proved to the foes of Christendom. The weapon had been bequeathed to him by a celebrated English outlaw named Hobbie Noble, who, having committed some deed for which he was in danger from justice, fled to Liddesdale, and became a follower, or rather a brother-in-arms, to the renowned Laird's Jock; till, venturing into England with a small escort, a faithless guide, and with a light single-handed sword instead of his ponderous brand, Hobbie Noble, attacked by superior numbers, was made prisoner and executed.

With this weapon, and by means of his own strength and address, the Laird's Jock maintained the reputation of the best swordsman on the Border side, and defeated or slew many who ventured to dispute with him the formidable title.

But years pass on with the strong and the brave as with the feeble and the timid. In process of time the Laird's Jock grew incapable of wielding his weapons, and finally of all active exertion, even of the most ordinary kind. The disabled champion became at length totally bedridden, and entirely dependent for his comfort on the pious duties of an only daughter, his perpetual attendant and companion.

Besides this dutiful child, the Laird's Jock had an only son, upon whom devolved the perilous task of leading the clan to battle, and maintaining the warlike renown of his native country, which was now disputed by the English upon many occasions. The young Armstrong was active, brave, and strong, and brought home from dangerous adventures many tokens of decided success. Still, the ancient chief conceived, as it would seem, that his son was scarce yet entitled by age and experience to be entrusted with the two-handed sword, by the use of which he had himself been so dreadfully distinguished.

At length an English champion, one of the name of Foster (if I rightly recollect), had the audacity to send a challenge to the best swordsman in Liddesdale; and young Armstrong, burning for chivalrous distinction, accepted the challenge.

The heart of the disabled old man swelled with joy when he heard that the challenge was passed and accepted, and the meeting fixed at a neutral spot, used as the place of rencontre upon such occasions, and which he himself had distinguished by numerous victories. He exulted so much in the conquest which he anticipated, that, to nerve his son to still bolder exertions, he conferred upon him, as champion of his clan and province, the celebrated weapon which he had hitherto retained in his own custody.

This was not all. When the day of combat arrived, the Laird's Jock, in spite of his daughter's affectionate remonstrances, determined, though he had not left his bed for two years, to be a personal witness of the duel. His will was still a law to his people, who bore him on their shoulders, wrapped in plaids and blankets, to the spot where the combat was to take place, and seated him on a fragment of rock, which is still called the Laird's Jock's stone. There he remained with eyes fixed on the lists or barrier, within which the champions were about to meet. His daughter, having done all she could for his accommodation, stood motionless beside him, divided between anxiety for his health, and for the event of the combat to her beloved brother. Ere yet the fight began, the old men gazed on their chief, now seen for the first time after several years, and sadly compared his altered features and wasted frame with the paragon of strength and manly beauty which they once remembered. The young men gazed on his large form and powerful make as upon some antediluvian giant who had survived the destruction of the Flood.

But the sound of the trumpets on both sides recalled the attention of every one to the lists, surrounded as they were by numbers of both nations eager to witness the event of the day. The combatants met in the lists. It is needless to describe the struggle: the Scottish champion fell. Foster, placing his foot on his antagonist, seized on the redoubted sword, so precious in the eyes of its aged owner, and brandished it over his head as a trophy of his conquest. The English shouted in triumph. But the despairing cry of the aged champion, who saw his country dishonoured, and his sword, long the terror of their race, in the possession of an Englishman, was heard high above the acclamations of victory. He seemed for an instant animated by all his wonted power; for he started from the rock on which he sat, and while the garments with which he had been invested fell from his wasted frame, and showed the ruins of his strength, he tossed his arms wildly to heaven, and uttered a cry of indignation, horror, and despair, which, tradition says, was heard to a preternatural distance, and resembled the cry of a dying lion more than a human sound.

His friends received him in their arms as he sank utterly exhausted by the effort, and bore him back to his castle in mute sorrow; while his daughter at once wept for her brother, and endeavoured to mitigate and soothe the despair of her father. But this was impossible; the old man's only tie to life was rent rudely asunder, and his heart had broken with it. The death of his son had no part in his sorrow. If he thought of him at all, it was as the degenerate boy through whom the honour of his country and clan had been lost; and he died in the course of three days, never even mentioning his name, but pouring out unintermitted lamentations for the loss of his noble sword.

I conceive that the moment when the disabled chief was roused into a last exertion by the agony of the moment is favourable to the object of a painter. He might obtain the full advantage of contrasting the form of the rugged old man, in the extremity of furious despair, with the softness and beauty of the female form. The fatal field might be thrown into perspective, so as to give full effect to these two principal figures, and with the single explanation that the piece represented a soldier beholding his son slain, and the honour of his country lost, the picture would be sufficiently intelligible at the first glance. If it was thought necessary to show more clearly the nature of the conflict, it might be indicated by the pennon of Saint George being displayed at one end of the lists, and that of Saint Andrew at the other.

I remain, sir,
Your obedient servant,
THE AUTHOR OF WAVERLEY.

4

WANDERING WILLIE'S TALE

Honest folks like me! How do ye ken whether I am honest, or what I am? I may be the deevil himself for what ye ken, for he has power to come disguised like an angel of light; and, besides, he is a prime fiddler. He played a sonata to Corelli, ye ken.'

There was something odd in this speech, and the tone in which it was said. It seemed as if my companion was not always in his constant mind, or that he was willing to try if he could frighten me. I laughed at the extravagance of his language, however, and asked him in reply if he was fool enough to believe that the foul fiend would play so silly a masquerade.

'Ye ken little about it—little about it,' said the old man, shaking his head and beard, and knitting his brows. 'I could tell ye something about that.'

What his wife mentioned of his being a tale-teller as well as a musician now occurred to me; and as, you know, I like tales of superstition, I begged to have a specimen of his talent as we went along.

'It is very true,' said the blind man, 'that when I am tired of scraping thairm or singing ballants I whiles make a tale serve the turn among the country bodies; and I have some fearsome anes, that make the auld carlines shake on the settle, and the bits o' bairns skirl on their minnies out frae their beds. But this that I am going to tell you was a thing that befell in our ain house in my father's time—that is, my father was then a hafflins callant; and I tell it to you, that it may be a lesson to you that are but a young thoughtless chap, wha ye draw up wi' on a lonely road; for muckle was the dool and care that came o' 't to my gudesire.'

He commenced his tale accordingly, in a distinct narrative tone of voice, which he raised and depressed with considerable skill; at times sinking almost into a whisper, and turning his clear but sightless eyeballs upon my face, as if it had been possible for him to witness the impression which his narrative made upon my features. I will not spare a syllable of it, although it be of the longest; so I make a dash—and begin:

Ye maun have heard of Sir Robert Redgauntlet of that ilk, who lived in these parts before the dear years. The country will lang mind him; and our fathers used to draw breath thick if ever they heard him named. He was out wi' the Hielandmen in Montrose's time; and again he was in the hills wi' Glencairn in the saxteen hundred and fifty-twa; and sae when King Charles the Second came in, wha was in sic favour as the laird of Redgauntlet? He was knighted at Lonon Court, wi' the king's ain sword; and being a red-hot prelatist, he came down here, rampauging like a lion, with commission of lieutenancy (and of lunacy, for what I ken), to put down a' the Whigs and Covenanters in the country. Wild wark they made of it; for the Whigs were as dour as the Cavaliers were fierce, and it was which should first tire the other. Redgauntlet was aye for the strong hand; and his name is kend as wide in the country as Claverhouse's or Tam Dalyell's. Glen, nor dargle, nor mountain, nor cave could hide the puir hill-folk when Redgauntlet was out with bugle and bloodhound after them, as if they had been sae mony deer. And, troth, when they fand them, they didna make muckle mair ceremony than a Hielandman wi' a roebuck. It was just, 'Will ye tak' the test?' If not—'Make ready—present—fire!' and there lay the recusant.

Far and wide was Sir Robert hated and feared. Men thought he had a direct compact with Satan; that he was proof against steel, and that bullets happed aff his buff-coat like hailstanes from a hearth; that he had a mear that would turn a hare on the side of Carrifra-gauns (a precipitous side of a mountain in Moffatdale); and muckle to the same purpose, of whilk mair anon. The best blessing they wared on him was, 'Deil scowp wi' Redgauntlet!' He wasna a bad master to his ain folk, though, and was weel aneugh liked by his tenants; and as for the lackeys and troopers that rade out wi' him to the persecutions, as the Whigs caa'd those killing-times, they wad hae drunken themsells blind to his health at ony time.

Now you are to ken that my gudesire lived on Redgauntlet's grund—they ca' the place Primrose Knowe. We had lived on the grund, and under the Redgauntlets, since the riding-days, and lang before. It was a pleasant bit; and, I think the air is callerer and fresher there than onywhere else in the country. It's a' deserted now; and I sat on the broken door-cheek three days since, and was glad I couldna see the plight the place was in—but that's a' wide o' the mark. There dwelt my gudesire, Steenie Steenson; a rambling, rattling chiel' he had been in his young days, and could play weel on the pipes; he was famous at 'hoopers and girders,' a' Cumberland couldna touch him at 'Jockie Lattin,' and he had the finest finger for the back-lilt between Berwick and Carlisle. The like o' Steenie wasna the sort that they made Whigs o'. And so he became a Tory, as they ca' it, which we now ca' Jacobites, just out of a kind of needcessity, that he might belang to some side or other. He had nae ill-will to the Whig bodies, and liked little to see the blude rin, though, being obliged to follow Sir Robert in hunting and hoisting, watching and warding, he saw muckle mischief, and maybe did some that he couldna avoid.

Now Steenie was a kind of favourite with his master, and kend a' the folk about the castle, and was often sent for to play the pipes when they were at their merriment. Auld Dougal MacCallum, the butler, that had followed Sir Robert through gude and ill, thick and thin, pool and stream, was specially fond of the pipes, and aye gae my gudesire his gude word wi' the laird; for Dougal could turn his master round his finger.

Weel, round came the Revolution, and it had like to hae broken the hearts baith of Dougal and his master. But the change was not a'thegether sae great as they feared and other folk thought for. The Whigs made an unco crawing what they wad do with their auld enemies, and in special wi' Sir Robert Redgauntlet. But there were ower-mony great folks dipped in the same doings to make a spick-and-span new warld. So Parliament passed it a' ower easy; and Sir Robert, bating that he was held to hunting foxes instead of Covenanters, remained just the man he was. His revel was as loud, and his hall as weel lighted, as ever it had been, though maybe he lacked the fines of the nonconformists, that used to come to stock his larder and cellar; for it is certain he began to be keener about the rents than his tenants used to find him before, and they behooved to be prompt to the rent-day, or else the laird wasna pleased. And he was sic an awsome body that naebody cared to anger him; for the oaths he swore, and the rage that he used to get into, and the looks that he put on made men sometimes think him a devil incarnate.

Weel, my gudesire was nae manager—no that he was a very great misguider—but he hadna the saving gift, and he got twa terms' rent in arrear. He got the first brash at Whitsunday put ower wi' fair word and piping; but when Martinmas came there was a summons from the grund officer to come wi' the rent on a day preceese, or else Steenie behooved to flit. Sair wark he had to get the siller; but he was weel freended, and at last he got the haill scraped thegether—a thousand merks. The maist of it was from a neighbour they caa'd Laurie Lapraik—a sly tod. Laurie had wealth o' gear, could hunt wi' the hound and rin wi' the hare, and be Whig or Tory, saunt or sinner, as the wind stood. He was a professor in the Revolution warld, but he liked an orra sough of the warld, and a tune on the pipes weel aneugh at a by-time; and, bune a', he thought he had gude security for the siller he len my gudesire ower the stocking at Primrose Knowe.

Away trots my gudesire to Redgauntlet Castle wi' a heavy purse and a light heart, glad to be out of the laird's danger. Weel, the first thing he learned at the castle was that Sir Robert had fretted himself into a fit of the gout because he did no appear before twelve o'clock. It wasna a'thegether for sake of the money, Dougal thought, but because he didna like to part wi' my gudesire aff the grund. Dougal was glad to see Steenie, and brought him into the great oak parlour; and there sat the laird his leesome lane, excepting that he had beside him a great, ill-favoured jackanape that was a special pet of his. A cankered beast it was, and mony an ill-natured trick it played; ill to please it was, and easily angered—ran about the haill castle, chattering and rowling, and pinching and biting folk, specially before ill weather, or disturbance in the state. Sir Robert caa'd it Major Weir, after the warlock that was burnt; and few folk liked either the name or the conditions of the creature—they thought there was something in it by ordinar—and my gudesire was not just easy in mind when the door shut on him, and he saw himself in the room wi' naebody but the laird, Dougal MacCallum, and the major—a thing that hadna chanced to him before.

Sir Robert sat, or, I should say, lay, in a great arm-chair, wi' his grand velvet gown, and his feet on a cradle, for he had baith gout and gravel, and his face looked as gash and ghastly as Satan's. Major Weir sat opposite to him, in a red-laced coat, and the laird's wig on his head; and aye as Sir Robert girned wi' pain, the jackanape girned too, like a sheep's head between a pair of tangs—an ill-faur'd, fearsome couple they were. The laird's buff-coat was hung on a pin behind him and his broadsword and his pistols within reach; for he keepit up the auld fashion of having the weapons ready, and a horse saddled day and night, just as he used to do when he was able to loup on horseback, and sway after ony of the hill-folk he could get speerings of. Some said it was for fear of the Whigs taking vengeance, but I judge it was just his auld custom—he wasna gine not fear onything. The rental-book, wi' its black cover and brass clasps, was lying beside him; and a book of sculduddery sangs was put betwixt the leaves, to keep it open at the place where it bore evidence against the goodman of Primrose Knowe, as behind the hand with his mails and duties. Sir Robert gave my gudesire a look, as if he would have withered his heart in his bosom. Ye maun ken he had a way of bending his brows that men saw the visible mark of a horseshoe in his forehead, deep-dinted, as if it had been stamped there.

'Are ye come light-handed, ye son of a toom whistle?' said Sir Robert. 'Zounds! If you are—'

My gudesire, with as gude a countenance as he could put on, made a leg, and placed the bag of money on the table wi' a dash, like a man that does something clever. The laird drew it to him hastily. 'Is all here, Steenie, man?'

'Your honour will find it right,' said my gudesire.

'Here, Dougal,' said the laird, 'gie Steenie a tass of brandy, till I count the siller and write the receipt.'

But they werena weel out of the room when Sir Robert gied a yelloch that garr'd the castle rock. Back ran Dougal; in flew the liverymen; yell on yell gied the laird, ilk ane mair awfu' than the ither. My gudesire knew not whether to stand or flee, but he ventured back into the parlour, where a' was gaun hirdie-girdie—naebody to say 'come in' or 'gae out.' Terribly the laird roared for cauld water to his feet, and wine to cool his throat; and 'Hell, hell, hell, and its flames', was aye the word in his mouth. They brought him water, and when they plunged his swoln feet into the tub, he cried out it was burning; and folks say that it *did* bubble and sparkle like a seething cauldron. He flung the cup at Dougal's head and said he had given him blood instead of Burgundy; and, sure aneugh, the lass washed clotted blood aff the carpet the neist day. The jackanape they caa'd Major Weir, it jibbered and cried as if it was mocking its master. My gudesire's head was like to turn; he forgot baith siller and receipt, and downstairs he banged; but, as he ran, the shrieks came fainter and fainter; there was a deep-drawn shivering groan, and word gaed through the castle that the laird was dead.

Weel, away came my gudesire wi' his finger in his mouth, and his best hope was that Dougal had seen the money-bag and heard the laird speak of writing the receipt. The young laird, now Sir John, came from Edinburgh to see things put to rights. Sir John and his father never 'greed weel. Sir John had been bred an advocate, and afterward sat in the last Scots Parliament and voted for the Union, having gotten, it was thought, a rug of the compensations—if his father could have come out of his grave he would have brained him for it on his awn hearthstane. Some thought it was easier counting with the auld rough knight than the fair-spoken young ane—but mair of that anon.

Dougal MacCallum, poor body, neither grat nor graned, but gaed about the house looking like a corpse, but directing, as was his duty, a' the order of the grand funeral. Now Dougal looked aye waur and waur when night was coming, and was aye the last to gang to his bed, whilk was in a little round just opposite the chamber of dais, whilk his master occupied while he was living, and where he now lay in state, as they can'd it, weeladay! The night before the funeral Dougal could keep his awn counsel nae longer; he came doun wi' his proud spirit, and fairly asked auld Hutcheon to sit in his room with him for an hour. When they were in the round, Dougal took a tass of brandy to himself, and gave another to Hutcheon, and wished him all health and lang life, and said that, for himself, he wasna lang for this warld; for that every night since Sir Robert's death his silver call had sounded from the state chamber just as it used to do at nights in his lifetime to call Dougal to help to turn him in his bed. Dougal said that being alone with the dead on that floor of the tower (for naebody cared to wake Sir Robert Redgauntlet like another corpse), he had never daured to answer the call, but that now his conscience checked him for neglecting his duty; for, 'though death breaks service,' said MacCallum, 'it shall never weak my service to Sir Robert; and I will answer his next whistle, so be you will stand by me, Hutcheon.'

Hutcheon had nae will to the wark, but he had stood by Dougal in battle and broil, and he wad not fail him at this pinch; so doun the carles sat ower a stoup of brandy, and Hutcheon, who was something of a clerk, would have read a chapter of the Bible; but Dougal would hear naething but a blaud of Davie Lindsay, whilk was the waur preparation.

When midnight came, and the house was quiet as the grave, sure enough the silver whistle sounded as sharp and shrill as if Sir Robert was blowing it; and up got the twa auld serving-men, and tottered into the room where the dead man lay. Hutcheon saw aneugh at the first glance; for there were torches in the room, which showed him the foul fiend, in his ain shape, sitting on the laird's coffin! Ower he couped as if he had been dead. He could not tell how lang he lay in a trance at the door, but when he gathered himself he cried on his neighbour, and getting nae answer raised the house, when Dougal was found lying dead within twa steps of the bed where his master's coffin was placed. As for the whistle, it was gane anes and aye; but mony a time was it heard at the top of the house on the bartizan, and amang the auld chimneys and turrets where the howlets have their nests. Sir John hushed the matter up, and the funeral passed over without mair bogie wark.

But when a' was ower, and the laird was beginning to settle his affairs, every tenant was called up for his arrears, and my gudesire for the full sum that stood against him in the rental-book. Weel, away he trots to the castle to tell his story, and there he is introduced to Sir John, sitting in his father's chair, in deep mourning, with weepers and hanging cravat, and a small walking-rapier by his side, instead of the auld broadsword that had a hunderweight of steel about it, what with blade, chape, and basket-hilt. I have heard their communings so often tauld ower that I almost think I was there mysell, though I couldna be born at the time. (In fact, Alan, my companion, mimicked, with a good deal of humour, the flattering, conciliating tone of the tenant's address and the hypocritical melancholy of the laird's reply. His grandfather, he said, had while he spoke, his eye fixed on the rental-book, as if it were a mastiff-dog that he was afraid would spring up and bite him.)

'I wuss ye joy, sir, of the head seat and the white loaf and the brid lairdship. Your father was a kind man to freends and followers; muckle grace to you, Sir John, to fill his shoon—his boots, I suld say, for he seldom wore shoon, unless it were muils when he had the gout.'__

'Ay, Steenie,' quoth the laird, sighing deeply, and putting his napkin to his een, 'his was a sudden call, and he will be missed in the country; no time to set his house in order—weel prepared Godward, no doubt, which is the root of the matter; but left us behind a tangled hesp to wind, Steenie. Hem! Hem!

We maun go to business, Steenie; much to do, and little time to do it in.'

Here he opened the fatal volume. I have heard of a thing they call Doomsday book—I am clear it has been a rental of back-ganging tenants.

'Stephen,' said Sir John, still in the same soft, sleekit tone of voice—'Stephen Stevenson, or Steenson, ye are down here for a year's rent behind the hand—due at last term.'

Stephen. Please your honour, Sir John, I paid it to your father.

Sir John. Ye took a receipt, then, doubtless, Stephen, and can produce it?

Stephen. Indeed, I hadna time, an it like your honour; for nae sooner had I set doun the siller, and just as his honour, Sir Robert, that's gaen, drew it ill him to count it and write out the receipt, he was ta'en wi' the pains that removed him.

'That was unlucky,' said Sir John, after a pause. 'But ye maybe paid it in the presence of somebody. I want but a *talis qualis* evidence, Stephen. I would go ower-strictly to work with no poor man.'

Stephen. Troth, Sir John, there was naebody in the room but Dougal MacCallum, the butler. But, as your honour kens, he has e'en followed his auld master.

'Very unlucky again, Stephen,' said Sir John, without altering his voice a single note. 'The man to whom ye paid the money is dead, and the man who witnessed the payment is dead too; and the siller, which should have been to the fore, is neither seen nor heard tell of in the repositories. How am I to believe a' this?'

Stephen. I dinna ken, your honour; but there is a bit memorandum note of the very coins, for, God help me! I had to borrow out of twenty purses; and I am sure that ilka man there set down will take his grit oath for what purpose I borrowed the money.

Sir John. I have little doubt ye *borrowed* the money, Steenie. It is the *payment* that I want to have proof of.

Stephen. The siller maun be about the house, Sir John. And since your honour never got it, and his honour that was canna have ta'en it wi' him, maybe some of the family may hae seen it.

Sir John. We will examine the servants, Stephen; that is but reasonable.

But lackey and lass, and page and groom, all denied stoutly that they had ever seen such a bag of money as my gudesire described. What saw waur, he had unluckily not mentioned to any living soul of them his purpose of paying his rent. Ae quean had noticed something under his arm, but she took it for the pipes.

Sir John Redgauntlet ordered the servants out of the room and then said to my gudesire, 'Now, Steenie, ye see ye have fair play; and, as I have little doubt ye ken better where to find the siller than ony other body, I beg in fair terms, and for your own sake, that you will end this fasherie; for, Stephen, ye maun pay or flit.'

'The Lord forgie your opinion,' said Stephen, driven almost to his wits' end—'I am an honest man.'

'So am I, Stephen,' said his honour; 'and so are all the folks in the house, I hope. But if there be a knave among us, it must be he that tells the story he cannot prove.' He paused, and then added, mair sternly: 'If I understand your trick, sir, you want to take advantage of some malicious reports concerning things in this family, and particularly respecting my father's sudden death, thereby to cheat me out of the money, and perhaps take away my character by insinuating that I have received the rent I am demanding. Where do you suppose the money to be? I insist upon knowing.'

My gudesire saw everything look so muckle against him

that he grew nearly desperate. However, he shifted from one foot to another, looked to every corner of the room, and made no answer.

'Speak out, sirrah,' said the laird, assuming a look of his father's, a very particular ane, which he had when he was angry—it seemed as if the wrinkles of his frown made that selfsame fearful shape of a horse's shoe in the middle of his brow; 'speak out, sir! I *will* know your thoughts; do you suppose that I have this money?'

'Far be it frae me to say so,' said Stephen.

'Do you charge any of my people with having taken it?'

'I wad be laith to charge them that may be innocent,' said my gudesire; 'and if there be any one that is guilty, I have nae proof.'

'Somewhere the money must be, if there is a word of truth in your story,' said Sir John; 'I ask where you think it is—and demand a correct answer!'

'In hell, if you *will* have my thoughts of it,' said my gudesire, driven to extremity—'in hell! with your father, his jackanape, and his silver whistle.'

Down the stairs he ran (for the parlour was nae place for him after such a word), and he heard the laird swearing blood and wounds behind him, as fast as ever did Sir Robert, and roaring for the bailie and the baron-officer.

Away rode my gudesire to his chief creditor (him they caa'd Laurie Lapraik), to try if he could make anything out of him; but when he tauld his story, he got the worst word in his wame—thief, beggar, and dyvour were the saftest terms; and to the boot of these hard terms, Laurie brought up the auld story of dipping his hand in the blood of God's saunts, just as if a tenant could have helped riding with the laird, and that a laird like Sir Robert Redgauntlet. My gudesire was, by this time, far beyond the bounds of patience, and, while he and

Laurie were at deil speed the liars, he was wanchancie aneugh to abuse Lapraik's doctrine as weel as the man, and said things that garr'd folks' flesh grue that heard them—he wasna just himsell, and he had lived wi' a wild set in his day.

At last they parted, and my gudesire was to ride hame through the wood of Pitmurkie, that is a' fou of black firs, as they say. I ken the wood, but the firs may be black or white for what I can tell. At the entry of the wood there is a wild common, and on the edge of the common a little lonely change-house, that was keepit then by an hostler wife,—they suld hae caa'd her Tibbie Faw,—and there puir Steenie cried for a mutchkin of brandy, for he had had no refreshment the haill day. Tibbie was earnest wi' him to take a bite of meat, but he couldna think o' 't, nor would he take his foot out of the stirrup, and took off the brandy, wholely at twa draughts, and named a toast at each. The first was, the memory of Sir Robert Redgauntlet, and may he never lie quiet in his grave till he had righted his poor bond-tenant; and the second was, a health to Man's Enemy, if he would but get him back the pock of siller, or tell him what came o' 't, for he saw the haill world was like to regard him as a thief and a cheat, and he took that waur than even the ruin of his house and hauld.

On he rode, little caring where. It was a dark night turned, and the trees made it yet darker, and he let the beast take its ain road through the wood; when all of a sudden, from tired and wearied that it was before, the nag began to spring and flee and stend, that my gudesire could hardly keep the saddle. Upon the whilk, a horseman, suddenly riding up beside him, said, 'That's a mettle beast of yours, freend; will you sell him?' So saying, he touched the horse's neck with his riding-wand, and it fell into its auld heigh-ho of a stumbling trot. 'But his spunk's soon out of him, I think,' continued the stranger, 'and that is like mony a man's courage, that thinks he wad do great things.'

My gudesire scarce listened to this, but spurred his horse, with 'Gude-e'en to you, freend.'

But it's like the stranger was ane that doesna lightly yield his point; for, ride as Steenie liked, he was aye beside him at the selfsame pace. At last my gudesire, Steenie Steenson, grew half angry, and, to say the truth, half feard.

'What is it that you want with me, freend?' he said. 'If ye be a robber, I have nae money; if ye be a leal man, wanting company, I have nae heart to mirth or speaking; and if ye want to ken the road, I scarce ken it mysell.'

'If you will tell me your grief,' said the stranger, 'I am one that, though I have been sair miscaa'd in the world, am the only hand for helping my freends.'

So my gudesire, to ease his ain heart, mair than from any hope of help, told him the story from beginning to end.

'It's a hard pinch,' said the stranger; 'but I think I can help you.'

'If you could lend me the money, sir, and take a lang day—I ken nae other help on earth,' said my gudesire.

'But there may be some under the earth,' said the stranger. 'Come, I'll be frank wi' you; I could lend you the money on bond, but you would maybe scruple my terms. Now I can tell you that your auld laird is disturbed in his grave by your curses and the wailing of your family, and if ye daur venture to go to see him, he will give you the receipt.'

My gudesire's hair stood on end at this proposal, but he thought his companion might be some humoursome chield that was trying to frighten him, and might end with lending him the money. Besides, he was bauld wi' brandy, and desperate wi' distress; and he said he had courage to go to the gate of hell, and a step farther, for that receipt. The stranger laughed.

Weel, they rode on through the thickest of the wood, when, all of a sudden, the horse stopped at the door of a great house; and, but that he knew the place was ten miles off, my father would have thought he was at Redgauntlet Castle. They rode into the outer courtyard, through the muckle faulding yetts, and aneath the auld portcullis; and the whole front of the house was lighted, and there were pipes and fiddles, and as much dancing and deray within as used to be at Sir Robert's house at Pace and Yule, and such high seasons. They lap off, and my gudesire, as seemed to him, fastened his horse to the very ring he had tied him to that morning when he gaed to wait on the young Sir John.

'God!' said my gudesire, 'if Sir Robert's death be but a dream!'

He knocked at the ha' door just as he was wont, and his auld acquaintance, Dougal MacCallum—just after his wont, too—came to open the door, and said, 'Piper Steenie, are ye there lad? Sir Robert has been crying for you.'

My gudesire was like a man in a dream—he looked for the stranger, but he was gane for the time. At last he just tried to say, 'Ha! Dougal Driveower, are you living? I thought ye had been dead.'

'Never fash yoursell wi' me,' said Dougal, 'but look to yoursell; and see ye tak' naething frae onybody here, neither meat, drink, or siller, except the receipt that is your ain.'

So saying, he led the way out through the halls and trances that were weel kend to my gudesire, and into the auld oak parlour; and there was as much singing of profane sangs, and birling of red wine, and blasphemy and sculduddery, as had ever been in Redgauntlet Castle when it was at the blythest.

But Lord take us in keeping! What a set of ghastly revellers there were that sat around that table! My gudesire kend mony that had long before gane to their place, for often had he piped to the most part in the hall of Redgauntlet. There was the fierce Middleton, and the dissolute Rothes, and the crafty Lauderdale;

and Dalyell, with his bald head and a beard to his girdle; and Earlshall, with Cameron's blude on his hand; and wild Bonshaw, that tied blessed Mr Cargill's limbs till the blude sprung; and Dumbarton Douglas, the twice turned traitor baith to country and king. There was the Bludy Advocate MacKenyie, who, for his worldly wit and wisdom, had been to the rest as a god. And there was Claverhouse, as beautiful as when he lived, with his long, dark, curled locks streaming down over his laced buff-coat, and with his left hand always on his right spule-blade, to hide the wound that the silver bullet had made. He sat apart from them all, and looked at them with a melancholy, haughty countenance; while the rest hallooed and sang and laughed, that the room rang. But their smiles were fearfully contorted from time to time; and their laughter passed into such wild sounds as made my gudesire's very nails grow blue, and chilled the marrow in his banes.

They that waited at the table were just the wicked serving-men and troopers that had done their work and cruel bidding on earth. There was the Lang Lad of the Nethertown, that helped to take Argyle; and the bishop's summoner, that they called the Deil's Rattlebag; and the wicked guardsmen in their laced coats; and the savage Highland Amorites, that shed blood like water; and mony a proud serving-man, haughty of heart and bloody of hand, cringing to the rich, and making them wickeder than they would be; grinding the poor to powder when the rich had broken them to fragments. And mony, mony mair were coming and ganging, a' as busy in their vocation as if they had been alive.

Sir Robert Redgauntlet, in the midst of a' this fearful riot, cried, wi' a voice like thunder, on Steenie Piper to come to the board-head where he was sitting, his legs stretched out before him, and swathed up with flannel, with his holster pistols aside him, while the great broadsword rested against his chair, just as my gudesire had seen him the last time upon earth; the very cushion for the jackanape was close to him, but the creature itself was not there—it wasna its hour, it's likely; for he heard them say, as he came forward, 'Is not the major come yet?' And another answered, 'The jackanape will be here betimes the morn.' And when my gudesire came forward, Sir Robert or his ghaist, or the deevil in his likeness, said, 'Weel, piper, hae ye settled wi' my son for the year's rent?'

With much ado my father gat breath to say that Sir John would not settle without his honour's receipt.

'Ye shall hae that for a tune of the pipes, Steenie,' said the appearance of Sir Robert—'play us up "Weel Hoddled, Luckie."'

Now this was a tune my gudesire learned frae a warlock, that heard it when they were worshipping Satan at their meetings; and my gudesire had sometimes played it at the ranting suppers in Redgauntlet Castle, but never very willingly; and now he grew cauld at the very name of it, and said, for excuse, he hadna his pipes wi' him.

'MacCallum, ye limb of Beelzebub,' said the fearfu' Sir Robert, 'bring Steenie the pipes that I am keeping for him!'

MacCallum brought a pair of pipes might have served the piper of Donald of the Isles. But he gave my gudesire a nudge as he offered them; and looking secretly and closely, Steenie saw that the chanter was of steel, and heated to a white heat; so he had fair warning not to trust his fingers with it. So he excused himsell again, and said he was faint and frightened, and had not wind aneugh to fill the bag.

'Then ye maun eat and drink, Steenie,' said the figure; 'for we do little else here; and it's ill speaking between a fou man and a fasting.' Now these were the very words that the bloody Earl of Douglas said to keep the king's messenger in hand while he cut the head off MacLellan of Bombie, at the Threave Castle; and put Steenie mair and mair on his guard.

So he spoke up like a man, and said he came neither to eat nor drink, nor make minstrelsy; but simply for his ain—to ken what was come o' the money he had paid, and to get a discharge for it; and he was so stout-hearted by this time that he charged Sir Robert for conscience's sake (he had no power to say the holy name), and as he hoped for peace and rest, to spread no snares for him, but just to give him his ain.

The appearance gnashed its teeth and laughed, but it took from a large pocket-book the receipt, and handed it to Steenie. 'There is your receipt, ye pitiful cur; and for the money, my dog-whelp of a son may go look for it in the Cat's Cradle.'

My gudesire uttered mony thanks, and was about to retire, when Sir Robert roared aloud, 'Stop, though, thou sack-doudling son of a—! I am not done with thee. HERE we do nothing for nothing; and you must return on this very day twelvemonth to pay your master the homage that you owe me for my protection.'

My father's tongue was loosed of a suddenty, and he said aloud, 'I refer myself to God's pleasure, and not to yours.'

He had no sooner uttered the word than all was dark around him; and he sank on the earth with such a sudden shock that he lost both breath and sense.

How lang Steenie lay there he could not tell; but when he came to himself he was lying in the auld kirkyard of Redgauntlet parochine, just at the door of the family aisle, and the scutcheon of the auld knight, Sir Robert, hanging over his head. There was a deep morning fog on grass and gravestane around him, and his horse was feeding quietly beside the minister's twa cows. Steenie would have thought the whole was a dream, but he had the receipt in his hand fairly written and signed by the auld laird; only the last letters of his name were a little disorderly, written like one seized with sudden pain.

Sorely troubled in his mind, he left that dreary place, rode through the mist to Redgauntlet Castle, and with much ado he got speech of the laird.

'Well, you dyvour bankrupt,' was the first word, 'have you brought me my rent?'

'No,' answered my gudesire, 'I have not; but I have brought your honour Sir Robert's receipt for it.'

'How, sirrah? Sir Robert's receipt! You told me he had not given you one.'

'Will your honour please to see if that bit line is right?'

Sir John looked at every line, and at every letter, with much attention; and at last at the date, which my gudesire had not observed—'From my appointed place,' he read, 'this twenty-fifth of November.'

'What! That is yesterday! Villain, thou must have gone to hell for this!'

'I got it from your honour's father; whether he be in heaven or hell, I know not,' said Steenie.

'I will debate you for a warlock to the Privy Council!' said Sir John. 'I will send you to your master, the devil, with the help of a tar-barrel and a torch!'

'I intend to debate mysell to the Presbytery,' said Steenie, 'and tell them all I have seen last night, whilk are things fitter for them to judge of than a borrel man like me.'

Sir John paused, composed himself, and desired to hear the full history; and my gudesire told it him from point to point, as I have told it you—neither more nor less.

Sir John was silent again for a long time, and at last he said, very composedly: 'Steenie, this story of yours concerns the honour of many a noble family besides mine; and if it be a leasing-making, to keep yourself out of my danger, the least you can expect is to have a red-hot iron driven through your tongue, and that will be as bad as scaulding your fingers wi' a red-hot chanter. But yet it may be true, Steenie; and if the money cast up, I shall not know what to think of it. But where shall we find the Cat's Cradle? There are cats enough about the old house, but I think they kitten without the ceremony of bed or cradle.'

'We were best ask Hutcheon,' said my gudesire; 'he kens a' the odd corners about as weel as—another serving-man that is now gane, and that I wad not like to name.'

Aweel, Hutcheon, when he was asked, told them that a ruinous turret lang disused, next to the clock-house, only accessible by a ladder, for the opening was on the outside, above the battlements, was called of old the Cat's Cradle.

'There will I go immediately,' said Sir John; and he took—with what purpose Heaven kens—one of his father's pistols from the hall table, where they had lain since the night he died, and hastened to the battlements.

It was a dangerous place to climb, for the ladder was auld and frail, and wanted ane or twa rounds. However, up got Sir John, and entered at the turret door, where his body stopped the only little light that was in the bit turret. Something flees at him wi' a vengeance, maist dang him back ower—bang! gaed the knight's pistol, and Hutcheon, that held the ladder, and my gudesire, that stood beside him, hears a loud skelloch. A minute after, Sir John flings the body of the jackanape down to them, and cries that the siller is fund, and that they should come up and help him. And there was the bag of siller sure aneaugh, and mony orra thing besides, that had been missing for mony a day. And Sir John, when he had riped the turret weel, led my gudesire into the dining-parlour, and took him by the hand, and spoke kindly to him, and said he was sorry he should have doubted his word, and that he would hereafter be a good master to him, to make amends.

'And now, Steenie,' said Sir John, 'although this vision of yours tends, on the whole, to my father's credit as an honest man, that he should, even after his death, desire to see justice done to a poor man like you, yet you are sensible that ill-dispositioned men might make bad constructions upon it concerning his soul's health. So, I think, we had better lay the haill dirdum on that ill-deedie creature, Major Weir, and say naething about your dream in the wood of Pitmurkie. You had taen ower-muckle brandy to be very certain about onything; and, Steenie, this receipt'—his hand shook while he held it out—'it's but a queer kind of document, and we will do best, I think, to put it quietly in the fire.'

'Od, but for as queer as it is, it's a' the voucher I have for my rent,' said my gudesire, who was afraid, it may be, of losing the benefit of Sir Robert's discharge.

'I will bear the contents to your credit in the rental-book, and give you a discharge under my own hand,' said Sir John, 'and that on the spot. And, Steenie, if you can hold your tongue about this matter, you shall sit, from this time downward, at an easier rent.'

'Mony thanks to your honour,' said Steenie, who saw easily in what corner the wind was; 'doubtless I will be conformable to all your honour's commands; only I would willingly speak wi' some powerful minister on the subject, for I do not like the sort of soumons of appointment whilk your honour's father—'

'Do not call the phantom my father!' said Sir John, interrupting him.

'Well then, the thing that was so like him,' said my gudesire; 'he spoke of my coming back to see him this time twelvemonth, and it's a weight on my conscience.'

'Aweel then,' said Sir John, 'if you be so much distressed in mind, you may speak to our minister of the parish; he is a douce man, regards the honour of our family, and the mair that he may look for some patronage from me.'

Wi' that, my father readily agreed that the receipt should

be burnt; and the laird threw it into the chimney with his ain hand. Burn it would not for them, though; but away it flew up the lum, wi' a lang train of sparks at its tail, and a hissing noise like a squib.

My gudesire gaed down to the manse, and the minister, when he had heard the story, said it was his real opinion that, though my gudesire had gane very far in tampering with dangerous matters, yet as he had refused the devil's arles (for such was the offer of meat and drink), and had refused to do homage by piping at his bidding, he hoped that, if he held a circumspect walk hereafter, Satan could take little advantage by what was come and gane. And, indeed, my gudesire, of his ain accord, lang forswore baith the pipes and the brandy—it was not even till the year was out, and the fatal day past, that he would so much as take the fiddle or drink usquebaugh or tippenny.

Sir John made up his story about the jackanape as he liked himself; and some believe till this day there was no more in the matter than the filching nature of the brute. Indeed, ye 'll no hinder some to thread that it was nane o' the auld Enemy that Dougal and Hutcheon saw in the laird's room, but only that wanchancie creature the major, capering on the coffin; and that, as to the blawing on the laird's whistle that was heard after he was dead, the filthy brute could do that as weel as the laird himself, if no better. But Heaven kens the truth, whilk first came out by the minister's wife, after Sir John and her ain gudeman were baith in the moulds. And then my gudesire, wha was failed in his limbs, but not in his judgment or memory,—at least nothing to speak of,—was obliged to tell the real narrative to his freends, for the credit of his good name. He might else have been charged for a warlock.

The shades of evening were growing thicker around us as my conductor finished his long narrative with this moral: 'You see, birkie, it is nae chancy thing to tak' a stranger traveller for a guide when you are in an uncouth land.'

'I should not have made that inference,' said I. 'Your grandfather's adventure was fortunate for himself, whom it saves from ruin and distress; and fortunate for his landlord.'

'Ay, but they had baith to sup the sauce o' 't sooner or later,' said Wandering Willie; 'what was fristed wasna forgiven. Sir John died before he was much over threescore; and it was just like a moment's illness. And for my gudesire, though he departed in fulness of life, yet there was my father, a yauld man of forty-five, fell down betwixt the stilts of his plough, and rase never again, and left nae bairn but me, a puir, sightless, fatherless, motherless creature, could neither work nor want. Things gaed weel aneugh at first; for Sir Regwald Redgauntlet, the only son of Sir John, and the oye of auld Sir Robert, and, wae's me! the last of the honourable house, took the farm aff our hands, and brought me into his household to have care of me. My head never settled since I lost him; and if I say another word about it, deil a bar will I have the heart to play the night. Look out, my gentle chap,' he resumed, in a different tone; 'ye should see the lights at Brokenburn Glen by this time.'

5

THE TWO DROVERS

It was the day after Doune Fair when my story commences. It had been a brisk market, several dealers had attended from the northern and midland counties in England, and English money had flown so merrily about as to gladden the hearts of the Highland farmers. Many large droves were about to set off for England, under the protection of their owners, or of the topsmen whom they employed in the tedious, laborious, and responsible office of driving the cattle for many hundred miles, from the market where they had been purchased, to the fields or farm-yards where they were to be fattened for the shambles.

The Highlanders in particular are masters of this difficult trade of driving, which seems to suit them as well as the trade of war. It affords exercise for all their habits of patient endurance and active exertion. They are required to know perfectly the drove-roads, which lie over the wildest tracts of the country, and to avoid as much as possible the highways, which distress the feet of the bullocks, and the turnpikes, which annoy the spirit of the drover; whereas on the broad green or grey track, which leads across the pathless moor, the herd not only move at ease and without taxation, but, if they mind their business, may pick up a mouthful of food by the way. At night, the drovers usually sleep along with their cattle, let the weather be what it will; and many of these hardymen do not once rest under a roof during a journey on foot from Lochaber to Lincolnshire. They are paid very highly, for the trust reposed is of the last importance, as it depends on their prudence, vigilance and honesty, whether the cattle reach the final market in good order, and afford a profit to the grazier. But as they maintain themselves at their own expense, they are especially economical in that particular. At the period we speak of, a Highland drover was victualled for his long and toilsome journey with a few handfulls of oatmeal and two or three onions, renewed from time to time, and a ram's horn filled with whisky, which he used regularly, but sparingly, every night and morning. His dirk, or *skene-dhu*, (*i.e.* black-knife,) so worn as to be concealed beneath the arm, or by the folds of the plaid, was his only weapon, excepting the cudgel with which he directed the movements of the cattle. A Highlander was never so happy as on these occasions. There was a variety in the whole journey, which exercised the Celt's curiosity and natural love of motion; there were the constant change of place and scene, the petty adventures incidental to the traffic, and the intercourse with the various farmers, graziers, and traders, intermingled with occasional merry-makings, not the less acceptable to Donald that they were void of expense;—and there was the consciousness of superior skill; for the Highlander, a child amongst flocks, is a prince amongst herds, and his natural habits induce him to disdain the shepherd's slothful life, so that he feels himself nowhere more at home than when following a gallant drove of his country cattle in the character of their guardian.

Of the number who left Doune in the morning, and with the purpose we have described, not a *Glunamie* of them all cocked his bonnet more briskly, or gartered his tartan hose under knee over a pair of more promising *spiogs*, (legs,) than did Robin Oig M'Combich, called familiarly Robin Oig, that is Young, or the Lesser, Robin. Though small of stature, as the epithet Oig implies, and not very strongly limbed, he was as light and alert as one of the deer of his mountains. He had an elasticity of step, which, in the course of a long march, made many a stout fellow envy him; and the manner in which he busked his plaid and adjusted his bonnet, argued a consciousness that so smart a John Highlandman as himself would not pass unnoticed among the Lowland lasses. The ruddy cheek, red lips, and white teeth, set off a countenance, which had gained by exposure to the weather a healthful and hardy rather than a rugged hue. If Robin Oig did not laugh, or even smile frequently, as indeed is not the practice among his countrymen, his bright eyes usually gleamed from under his bonnet with an expression of cheerfulness ready to be turned into mirth. The departure of Robin Oig was an incident in the little town, in and near which he had many friends, male and female. He was a topping person in his way, transacted considerable business on his own behalf, and was intrusted by the best farmers in the Highlands, in reference to any other drover in that district. He might have increased his business to any extent had he condescended to manage it by deputy; but except a lad or two, sister's sons of his own, Robin rejected the idea of assistance, conscious, perhaps, how much his reputation depended upon his attending in person to the practical discharge of his duty in every instance.

He remained, therefore, contented with the highest premium given to persons of his description, and comforted himself with the hopes that few journeys to England might enable him to conduct business on his own account, in a manner becoming his birth. For Robin Oig's father, Lachlan M'Combich, (or *son of my friend*, his actual clan-surname being M'Gregor,) had been so called by the celebrated Rob Roy, because of the particular friendship which had subsisted between the grandsire of Robin and that renowned cateran. Some people even say, that Robin Oig derived his Christian name from one as renowned in the wilds of Lochlomond as ever was his namesake Robin Hood, in the precincts of merry Sherwood. 'Of such ancestry,' as James Boswell says, 'who would not be proud?' Robin Oig was proud accordingly; but his frequent visits to England and to the Lowlands had given him tact enough to know that pretensions, which still gave him a little right to distinction in his own lonely glen, might be both obnoxious and ridiculous if preferred elsewhere. The pride of birth, therefore, was like the miser's treasure, the secret subject of his contemplation, but never exhibited to strangers as a subject of boasting.

Many were the words of gratulation and good-luck which were bestowed on Robin Oig. The judges commended his drove, especially Robin's own property, which were the best of them. Some thrust out their snuff-mulls for the parting pinch—others tendered the *doch-an-dorrach*, or parting cup. All cried—'Good-luck travel out with you and come home with you.—Give you luck in the Saxon market—brave notes in the *leabhar-dhu*,' (black pocketbook,) 'and plenty of English gold in the *sporran*,' (pouch of goat-skin.)

The bonny lasses made their adieus more modestly, and more than one, it was said, would have given her best brooch to be certain that it was upon her that his eye last rested as he turned towards the road.

Robin Oig had just given the preliminary 'Hoo-hoo!' to urge forward the loiterers of the drove, when there was a cry behind him. 'Stay, Robin—bide a blink. Here is Janet of Tomahourich—auld Janet, your father's sister.'

'Plague on her, for an auld Highland witch and spaewife,' said a farmer from the Carse of Stirling; 'she'll cast some of her cantrips on the cattle.' 'She canna do that,' said another sapient of the same profession—'Robin Oig is no the lad to leave any of them, without tying Saint Mungo's knot on their tails, and that will put to her speed the best witch that ever flew over Dimayet upon a broomstick.'

It may not be indifferent to the reader to know that the Highland cattle are peculiarly liable to be taken, or infected, by spells and witchcraft, which judicious people guard against by knitting knots of peculiar complexity on the tuft of hair which terminates the animal's tail.

But the old woman who was the object of the farmer's suspicion seemed only busied about the drover, without paying any attention to the drove.

Robin, on the contrary, appeared rather impatient of her presence.

'What auld-world fancy,' he said, 'has brought you so early from the ingle-side this morning, Muhme? I am sure I bid you good-even, and had your God-speed, last night.'

'And left me more siller than the useless old woman will use till you come back again, bird of my bosom,' said the sibyl. 'But it is little I would care for the food that nourishes me, or the fire that warms me, or for God's blessed sun itself, if aught but weal should happen to the grandson of my father. So let me walk the *deasil* round you, that you may go safe out into the far foreign land, and come safe home.'

Robin Oig stopped, half embarrassed, half laughing, and signing to those around that he only complied with the old woman to soothe her humour. In the meantime, she traced around him, with wavering steps, the propitiation, which some have thought has been derived from the Druidical mythology. It consists, as is well known, in the person who makes the *deasil* walking three times round the person who is the object of the ceremony, taking care to move according to the course of the sun.

At once, however, she stopped short, and exclaimed, in a

voice of alarm and horror, 'Grandson of my father, there is blood on your hand.'

'Hush, for God's sake, aunt,' said Robin Oig; 'you will bring more trouble on yourself with this Taishataragh' (second sight) 'than you will be able to get out of for many a day.'

The old woman only repeated, with a ghastly look, 'There is blood on your hand, and it is English blood. The blood of the Gael is richer and redder. Let us see—let us———'

Ere Robin Oig could prevent her, which, indeed, could only have been by positive violence, so hasty and peremptory were her proceedings, she had drawn from his side the dirk which lodged in the folds of his plaid, and held it up, exclaiming, although the weapon gleamed clear and bright in the sun, 'Blood, blood—Saxon blood again. Robin Oig M'Combich, go not this day to England!'

'Prutt, trutt,' answered Robin Oig, 'that will never do neither—it would be next thing to running the country. For shame, Muhme—give me the dirk. You cannot tell by the colour the difference betwixt the blood of a black bullock and a white one, and you speak of knowing Saxon from Gaelic blood. All men have their blood from Adam, Muhme. Give me my skene-dhu, and let me go on my road. I should have been half way to Stirling brig by this time—Give me my dirk, and let me go.'

'Never will I give it to you,' said the old woman—'Never will I quit my hold on your plaid, unless you promise me not to wear that unhappy weapon.'

The women around him urged him also, saying few of his aunt's words fell to the ground; and as the Lowland farmers continued to look moodily on the scene, Robin Oig determined to close it at any sacrifice.

'Well, then,' said the young drover, giving the scabbard of the weapon to Hugh Morrison, 'you Lowlanders care nothing for these treats. Keep my dirk for me. I cannot give it you, because it was my father's; but your drove follows ours, and I am content it should be in your keeping, not in mine.—Will this do, Muhme?'

'It must,' said the old woman—'that is, if the Lowlander is mad enough to carry the knife.'

The strong westlandman laughed aloud.

'Goodwife,' said he, 'I am Hugh Morrison from Glenae, come of the Manly Morrisons of auld langsyne, that never took short weapon against a man in their lives. And neither needed they: They had their broadswords, and I have this bit supple,' showing a formidable cudgel—'for dirking ower the board, I leave that to John Highlandman.—Ye needna snort, none of you Highlanders, and you in especial, Robin. I'll keep the bit knife, if you are feared for the auld spaewife's tale, and give it back to you whenever you want it.'

Robin was not particularly pleased with some part of Hugh Morrison's speech; but he had learned in his travels more patience than belonged to his Highland constitution originally, and he accepted the service of the descendant of the Manly Morrisons, without finding fault with the rather depreciating manner in which it was offered.

'If he had not had his morning in his bead, and been but a Dumfries-shire hog into the boot, he would have spoken more like a gentleman. But you cannot have more of a sow than a grumph. It's shame my father's knife should ever slash a haggis for the like of him,'

Thus saying, (but saying it in Gaelic,) Robin drove on his cattle, and waved farewell to all behind him. He was in the greater haste, because he expected to join at Falkirk a comrade and brother in profession, with whom he proposed to travel in company.

Robin Oig's chosen friend was a young Englishman, Harry Wakefield by name, well known at every northern market, and in his way as much famed and honoured as our Highland driver of bullocks. He was nearly six feet high, gallantly formed to keep the rounds at Smithfield, or maintain the ring at a wrestling match; and although he might have been overmatched, perhaps, among the regular professors of the Fancy, yet, as a yokel or rustic, or a chance customer, he was able to give a bellyful to any amateur of the pugilistic art. Doncaster races saw him in his glory, betting his guinea, and generally successfully; nor was there a main fought in Yorkshire, the feeders being persons of celebrity, at which he was not to be seen if business permitted. But though a *sprack* lad, and fond of pleasure and its haunts, Harry Wakefield was steady, and not the cautious Robin Oig M'Combich himself was more attentive to the main chance. His holidays were holidays indeed; but his days of work were dedicated to steady and persevering labour. In countenance and temper, Wakefield was the model of Old England's merry yeomen, whose clothyard shafts, in so many hundred battles, asserted her superiority over the nations, and whose good sabres, in our own time, are her cheapest and most assured defence. His mirth was readily excited; for, strong in limb and constitution, and fortunate in circumstances, he was disposed to be pleased with every thing about him; and such difficulties as he might occasionally encounter, were, to a man of his energy, rather matter of amusement than serious annoyance. With all the merits of a sanguine temper, our young English drover was not without his defects. He was irascible, sometimes to the verge of being quarrelsome; and perhaps not the less inclined to bring his disputes to a pugilistic decision, because he found few antagonists able to stand up to him in the boxing ring.

It is difficult to say how Harry Wakefield and Robin Oig first became intimates; but it is certain a close acquaintance had taken place betwixt them, although they had apparently few common subjects of conversation or of interest, so soon as their talk ceased to be of bullocks. Robin Oig, indeed, spoke the English language rather imperfectly upon any other topics but stots and kyloes, and Harry Wakefield could never bring his broad Yorkshire tongue to utter a single word of Gaelic. It was in vain Robin spent a whole morning, during a walk over Minch Moor, in attempting to teach his companion to utter, with true precision, the shibboleth *Llhu*, which is the Gaelic for a calf. From Traquair to Murder-cairn, the hill rung with the discordant attempts of the Saxon upon the unmanageable monosyllable, and the heartfelt laugh which followed every failure. They had, however, better modes of awakening the echoes; for Wakefield could sing many a ditty to the praise of Moll, Susan, and Cicely, and Robin Oig had a particular gift at whistling interminable pibrochs through all their involutions, and what was more agreeable to his companion's southern ear, knew many of the northern airs, both lively and pathetic, to which Wakefield learned to pipe a bass. Thus, though Robin could hardly have comprehended his companion's stories about horse-racing, and cock-fighting, or fox-hunting, and although his own legends of clan-fights and *creaghs*, varied with talk of Highland goblins and fairy folk, would have been caviare to his companion, they contrived nevertheless to find a degree of pleasure in each other's company, which had for three years back induced them to join company and travel together, when the direction of their journey permitted. Each, indeed, found his advantage in this companionship; for where could the Englishman have found a guide through the Western Highlands like Robin Oig M'Combich? and when they were on what Harry called the *right* side of the Border, his patronage, which was extensive, and his purse, which was heavy, were at all times at the service of his Highland friend, and on many occasions his liberality did him genuine yeoman's service.

> *Were ever two such loving friends*
> *How could they disagree?*
> *O thus it was, he loved him dear,*
> *And thought how to requite him,*
> *And having no friend left but he,*
> *He did resolve to fight him.*
>   –Duke upon Duke.

The pair of friends had traversed with their usual cordiality the grassy wilds of Liddesdale, and crossed the opposite part of Cumberland, emphatically called The Waste. In these solitary regions, the cattle under the charge of our drovers derived their subsistence chiefly by picking their food as they went along the drove-road, or sometimes by the tempting opportunity of a *start and owerloup*, or invasion of the neighbouring pasture, where an occasion presented itself. But now the scene changed before them; they were descending towards a fertile and enclosed country, where no such liberties could be taken with impunity, or without a previous arrangement and bargain with the possessors of the ground. This was more especially the case, as a great northern fair was upon the eve of taking place, where both the Scotch and English drover expected to dispose of a part of their cattle, which it was desirable to produce in the market, rested and in good order. Fields were therefore difficult to be obtained, and only upon high terms. This necessity occasioned a temporary separation betwixt the two friends, who went to bargain, each as he could, for the separate accommodation of his herd. Unhappily it chanced that both of them, unknown to each other, thought of bargaining for the ground they wanted on the property of a country gentleman of some fortune, whose estate lay in the neighbourhood. The English drover applied to the bailiff on the property, who was known to him. It chanced that the Cumbrian Squire, who had entertained some suspicions of his manager's honesty, was taking occasional measures to ascertain how far they were well founded, and had desired that any inquiries about his enclosures, with a view to occupy them for a temporary purpose, should be referred to himself. As however, Mr Ireby had gone the day before upon a journey of some miles distance to the northward, the bailiff chose to consider the check upon his full powers as for the time removed, and concluded that be should best consult his master's interest, and perhaps his own, in making an agreement with Harry Wakefield. Meanwhile, ignorant of what his comrade was doing, Robin Oig, on his side, chanced to be overtaken by a good-looking smart little man upon a pony, most knowingly bogged and cropped, as was then the fashion, the rider wearing tight leather breeches, and long-necked bright spurs. This cavalier asked one or two pertinent questions about markets and the price of stock. So Robin, seeing him a well-judging civil gentleman, took the freedom to ask him whether he could let him know if there was any grass-land to be let in that neighbourhood, for the temporary accommodation of his drove. He could not have put the question to more willing ears. The gentleman of the buckskins was the proprietor, with whose bailiff Harry Wakefield had dealt, or was in the act of dealing.

'Thou art in good luck, my canny Scot,' said Mr Ireby, 'to have spoken to me, for I see thy cattle have done their day's work, and I have at my disposal the only field within three miles that is to be let in these parts.'

'The drove can pe gang two, three, four miles very pratty weel indeed'—said the cautious Highlander; 'put what would his honour pe axing for the peasts pe the head, if she was to tak the park for twa or three days?'

'We won't differ, Sawney, if you let me have six stots for winterers, in the way of reason.'

'And which peasts wad your honour pe for having?'

'Why—let me see—the two black—the dun one—yon doddy—him with the twisted horn—the brockit—How much by the head?'

'Ah,' said Robin, 'your honour is a shudge—a real shudge—I couldna have set off the pest six peasts petter mysell, me that ken them as if they were my pairns, puir things.'

'Well, how much per head, Sawney,' continued Mr Ireby.

'It was high markets at Doune and Falkirk,' answered Robin.

And thus the conversation proceeded, until they had agreed on the *prix juste* for the bullocks, the Squire throwing in the temporary accommodation of the enclosure for the cattle into the boot, and Robin making, as he thought, a very good bargain, provided the grass was but tolerable. The Squire walked his pony alongside of the drove, partly to show him the way, and see him put into possession of the field, and partly to learn the latest news of the northern markets.

They arrived at the field, and the pasture seemed excellent. But what was their surprise when they saw the bailiff quietly inducting the cattle of Harry Wakefield into the grassy Goshen which had just been assigned to those of Robin Oig M'Combich by the proprietor himself! Squire Ireby set spurs to his horse, dashed up to his servant, and learning what had passed between the parties, briefly informed the English drover that his bailiff had let the ground without his authority, and that he might seek grass for his cattle wherever he would, since he was to get none there. At the same time he rebuked his servant severely for having transgressed his commands, and ordered him instantly to assist in ejecting the hungry and weary cattle of Harry Wakefield, which were just beginning to enjoy a meal of unusual plenty, and to introduce those of his comrade, whom the English drover now began to consider as a rival.

The feelings which arose in Wakefield's mind would have

induced him to resist Mr Ireby's decision; but every Englishman has a tolerably accurate sense of law and justice, and John Fleecebumpkin, the bailiff, having acknowledged that he had exceeded his commission, Wakefield saw nothing else for it than to collect his hungry and disappointed charge, and drive them on to seek quarters elsewhere. Robin Oig saw what had happened with regret, and hastened to offer to his English friend to share with him the disputed possession. But Wakefield's pride was severely hurt, and he answered disdainfully, 'Take it all, man—take it all—never make two bites of a cherry—thou canst talk over the gentry, and blear a plain man's eye—Out upon you, man—I would not kiss any man's dirty latchets for leave to bake in his oven.'

Robin Oig, sorry but not surprised at his comrade's displeasure, hastened to entreat his friend to wait but an hour till he had gone to the Squire's house to receive payment for the cattle he had sold, and he would come back and help him to drive the cattle into some convenient place of rest, and explain to him the whole mistake they had both of them fallen into. But the Englishman continued indignant: 'Thou hast been selling, hast thou? Ay, ay—thou is a cunning lad for kenning the hours of bargaining. Go to the devil with thyself, for I will neer see thy fause loon's visage again—thou should be ashamed to look me in the face.'

'I am ashamed to look no man in the face,' said Robin Oig, something moved; 'and, moreover, I will look you in the face this blessed day, if you will bide at the Clachan down yonder.'

'Mayhap you had as well keep away,' said his comrade; and turning his back on his former friend, he collected his unwilling associates, assisted by the bailiff, who took some real and some affected interest in seeing Wakefield accommodated.

After spending some time in negotiating with more than one of the neighbouring farmers, who could not, or would not, afford the accommodation desired, Henry Wakefield at last, and in his necessity, accomplished his point by means of the landlord of the alehouse at which Robin Oig and he had agreed to pass the night, when they first separated from each other. Mine host was content to let him turn his cattle on a piece of barren moor, at a price little less than the bailiff had asked for the disputed enclosure; and the wretchedness of the pasture, as well as the price paid for it, were set down as exaggerations of the breach of faith and friendship of his Scottish crony. This turn of Wakefield's passions was encouraged by the bailiff, (who had his own reasons for being offended against poor Robin, as having been the unwitting cause of his falling into disgrace with his master,) as well as by the innkeeper, and two or three chance guests, who stimulated the drover in his resentment against his quondam associate,—some from the ancient grudge against the Scots, which, when it exists anywhere, is to be found lurking in the Border counties, and some from the general love of mischief, which characterises mankind in all ranks of life, to the honour of Adam's children be it spoken. Good John Barleycorn also, who always heightens and exaggerates the prevailing passions, be they angry or kindly, was not wanting in his offices on this occasion; and confusion to false friends and hard masters, was pledged in more than one tankard.

In the meanwhile Mr Ireby found some amusement in detaining the northern drover at his ancient hall. He caused a cold round of beef to be placed before the Scot in the butler's pantry, together with a foaming tankard of home-brewed, and took pleasure in seeing the hearty appetite with which these unwonted edibles were discussed by Robin Oig M'Combich. The Squire himself lighting his pipe, compounded between his patrician dignity and his love of agricultural gossip, by walking up and down while he conversed with his guest.

'I passed another drove,' said the Squire, with one of

your countrymen behind them—they were something less beasts than your drove, doddies most of them—a big man was with them—none of your kilts though, but a decent pair of breeches—D'ye know who he may be?'

'Hout aye—that might, could, and would be Hughie Morrison—I didna think he could hae peen sae weel up. He has made a day on us; but his Argyleshires will have wearied shanks. How far was he pehind?'

'I think about six or seven miles,' answered the Squire, 'for I passed them at the Christenbury Crag, and I overtook you at the Hollan Bush. If his beasts be leg-weary, he will be maybe selling bargains.'

'Na, na, Hughie Morrison is no the man for pargains—ye maun come to some Highland body like Robin Oig hersell for the like of these—put I maun pe wishing you goot night, and twenty of them let alane ane, and I maun down to the Clachan to see if the lad Harry Waakfelt is out of his humdudgeons yet.'

The party at the alehouse were still in full talk, and the treachery of Robin Oig still the theme of conversation, when the supposed culprit entered the apartment. His arrival, as usually happens in such a case, put an instant stop to the discussion of which he had furnished the subject, and he was received by the company assembled with that chilling silence, which, more than a thousand exclamations, tells an intruder that he is unwelcome. Surprised and offended, but not appalled by the reception which he experienced, Robin entered with an undaunted and even a haughty air, attempted no greeting, as he saw he was received with none, and placed himself by the side of the fire, a little apart from a table, at which Harry Wakefield, the bailiff, and two or three other persons, were seated. The ample Cumbrian kitchen would have afforded plenty of room, even for a larger separation.

Robin thus seated, proceeded to light his pipe, and call for a pint of twopenny.

'We have no twopence ale,' answered Ralph Heskett the landlord; 'but as thou find'st thy own tobacco, it's like thou mayst find thy own liquor too—it's the wont of thy country, I wot.'

'Shame, goodman,' said the landlady, a blithe bustling housewife, hastening herself to supply the guest with liquor—'Thou knowest well enow what the strange man wants, and it's thy trade to be civil, man. Thou shouldst know, that if the Scot likes a small pot, he pays a sure penny.'

Without taking any notice of this nuptial dialogue, the Highlander took the flagon in his hand, and addressing the company generally, drank the interesting toast of 'Good markets,' to the party assembled.

'The better that the wind blew fewer dealers from the north,' said one of the farmers, 'and fewer Highland runts to eat up the English meadows.'

'Saul of my pody, put you are wrang there, my friend,' answered Robin, with composure; 'it is your fat Englishmen that eat up our Scots cattle, puir things.'

'I wish there was a summat to eat up their drovers,' said another; 'a plain Englishman canna make bread within a kenning of them.'

'Or an honest servant keep his master's favour but they will come sliding in between him and the sunshine,' said the bailiff.

'If these pe jokes,' said Robin Oig, with the same composure, 'there is ower many jokes upon one man.'

'It is no joke, but downright earnest,' said the bailiff. 'Harkye, Mr Robin Ogg, or whatever is your name, it's right we should tell you that we are all of one opinion, and that is, that you, Mr Robin Ogg, have behaved to our friend Mr Harry Wakefield here, like a raff and a blackguard.'

'Nae doubt, nae doubt,' answered Robin, with great composure; 'and you are a set of very pretty judges, for whose prains or pehaviour I wad not gie a pinch of sneeshing. If Mr Harry Waakfelt kens where he is wronged, he kens where he may be righted.'

'He speaks truth,' said Wakefield, who had listened to what passed, divided between the offence which he had taken at Robin's late behaviour, and the revival of his habitual feelings of regard.

He now rose, and went towards Robin, who got up from his seat as he approached, and held out his hand.

'That's right, Harry—go it—serve him out,' resounded on all sides—'tip him the nailer—show him the mill.'

'Hold your peace all of you, and be———,' said Wakefield; and then addressing his comrade, he took him by the extended band, with something alike of respect and defiance. 'Robin,' he said, 'thou hast used me ill enough this day; but if you mean, like a frank fellow, to shake hands, and take a tussle for love on the sod, why I'll forgie thee, man, and we shall be better friends than ever.'

'And would it not pe petter to pe cood friends without more of the matter?' said Robin; 'we will be much petter friendships with our panes hale than proken.'

Harry Wakefield dropped the band of his friend, or rather threw it from him.

'I did not think I had been keeping company for three years with a coward.'

'Coward pelongs to none of my name,' said Robin, whose eyes began to kindle, but keeping the command of his temper. 'It was no coward's legs or hands, Harry Waakfelt, that drew you out of the fords of Frew, when you was drifting ower the plack rock, and every eel in the river expected his share of you.'

'And that is true enough, too,' said the Englishman, struck by the appeal.

'Adzooks!' exclaimed the bailiff—'sure Harry Wakefield, the nattiest lad at Whitson Tryste, Wooler Fair, Carlisle Sands, or Stagshaw Bank, is not going to show white feather? Ah, this comes of living so long with kilts and bonnets—men forget the use of their daddies.'

'I may teach you, Master Fleecebumpkin, that I have not lost the use of mine,' said Wakefield and then went on. 'This will never do, Robin. We must have a turn-up, or we shall be the talk of the country-side. I'll be d———d if I hurt thee—I'll put on the gloves gin thou like. Come, stand forward like a man.'

'To be peaten like a dog,' said Robin; 'is there any reason in that? If you think I have done you wrong, I'll go before your shudge, though I neither know his law nor his language.'

A general cry of 'No, no—no law, no lawyer! a bellyful and be friends,' was echoed by the bystanders.

'But,' continued Robin, 'if I am to fight, I have no skill to fight like a jackanapes, with hands and nails.'

'How would you fight then?' said his antagonist; 'though I am thinking it would be hard to bring you to the scratch anyhow.'

'I would fight with proadswords, and sink point on the first plood drawn—like a gentlemans.'

A loud shout of laughter followed the proposal, which indeed had rather escaped from poor Robin's swelling heart, than been the dictate of his sober judgment.

'Gentleman, quotha!' was echoed on all sides, with a shout of unextinguishable laughter; 'a very pretty gentleman, God wot—Canst get two swords for the gentleman to fight with, Ralph Heskett?'

'No, but I can send to the armoury at Carlisle, and lend them two forks, to be making shift with in the meantime.'

'Tush, man,' said another, 'the bonny Scots come into the world with the blue bonnet on their heads, and dirk and pistol at their belt.'

'Best send post,' said Mr Fleecebumpkin, 'to the Squire of Corby Castle, to come and stand second to the gentleman.'

In the midst of this torrent of general ridicule, the Highlander instinctively griped beneath the folds of his plaid, 'But it's better not,' he said in his own language. 'A hundred curses on the swilie-eaters, who know neither decency nor civility!'

'Make room, the pack of you,' he said advancing to the door.

But his former friend interposed his sturdy bulk, and opposed his leaving the house; and when Robin Oig attempted to make his way by force, he hit him down on the floor, with as much ease as a boy bowls down a nine-pin.

'A ring, a ring!' was now shouted, until the dark rafters, and the hams that hung on them, trembled again, and the very platters on the *bink* clattered against each other. 'Well done, Harry'—'Give it him home Harry'—'Take care of him now-he sees his own blood!'

Such were the exclamations, while the Highlander, starting from the ground, all his coldness and caution lost in frantic rage, sprung at his antagonist with the fury, the activity, and the vindictive purpose of an incensed tiger-cat. But when could rage encounter science and temper? Robin Oig again went down in the unequal contest; and as the blow was necessarily a severe one, he lay motionless on the floor of the kitchen. The landlady ran to offer some aid, but Mr Fleecebumpkin would not permit her to approach.

'Let him alone,' he said, 'he will come to within time, and come up to the scratch again. He has not got half his broth yet.'

'He has got all I mean to give him, though,' said his

antagonist, whose heart began to relent towards his old associate; 'and I would rather by half give the rest to yourself, Mr Fleecebumpkin, for you pretend to know a thing or two, and Robin had not art enough even to peel before setting to, but fought with his plaid dangling about him.—Stand up, Robin, my man! all friends now; and let me hear the man that will speak a word against you, or your country, for your sake.'

Robin Oig was still under the dominion of his passion, and eager to renew the onset; but being withheld on the one side by the peace-making Dame Heskett, and on the other, aware that Wakefield no longer meant to renew the combat, his fury sunk into gloomy sullenness.

'Come, come, never grudge so much at it, man,' said the brave-spirited Englishman, with the placability of his country, 'shake hands, and we will be better friends than ever.'

'Friends!' exclaimed Robin Oig with strong emphasis—'friends!—Never. Look to yourself, Harry Waakfelt.'

'Then the curse of Cromwell on your proud Scots stomach, as the man says in the play, and you may do your worst, and be d—; for one man can say nothing more to another after a tussle, than that he is sorry for it.'

On these terms the friends parted; Robin Oig drew out, in silence, a piece of money, threw it on the table, and then left the alehouse. But turning at the door, he shook his hand at Wakefield, pointing with his forefinger upwards, in a manner which might imply either a threat or a caution. He then disappeared in the moonlight.

Some words passed after his departure, between the bailiff, who piqued himself on being a little of a bully, and Harry Wakefield, who, with generous inconsistency, was now not indisposed to begin a new combat in defence of Robin Oig's reputation, 'although he could not use his daddles like an Englishman, as it did not come natural to him.' But Dame

Heskett prevented this second quarrel from coming to a head by her peremptory interference. 'There should be no more fighting in her house,' she said; 'there had been too much already.—And you, Mr Wakefield, may live to learn,' she added, 'what it is to make a deadly enemy out of a good friend.'

'Pshaw, dame! Robin Oig is an honest fellow, and will never keep malice.'

'Do not trust to that—you do not know the dour temper of the Scots, though you have dealt with them so often. I have a right to know them, my mother being a Scot.'

'And so is well seen on her daughter,' said Ralph Heskett.

This nuptial sarcasm gave the discourse another turn; fresh customers entered the tap-room or kitchen, and others left it. The conversation turned on the expected markets, and the report of prices from different parts both of Scotland and England—treaties were commenced, and Harry Wakefield was lucky enough to find a chap for a part of his drove, and at a very considerable profit; an event of consequence more than sufficient to blot out all remembrances of the unpleasant scuffle in the earlier part of the day. But there remained one party from whose mind that recollection could not have been wiped away by the possession of every head of cattle betwixt Esk and Eden.

This was Robin Oig M'Combich.—'That I should have had no weapon,' he said, 'and for the first time in my life!—Blighted be the tongue that bids the Highlander part with the dirk—the dirk—ha! the English blood!—My Muhme's word—when did her word fall to the ground?'

The recollection of the fatal prophecy confirmed the deadly intention which instantly sprang up in his mind.

'Ha! Morrison cannot be many miles behind; and if it were an hundred, what then!'

His impetuous spirit had now a fixed purpose and motive

of action, and he turned the light foot of his country towards the wilds, through which he knew, by Mr Ireby's report, that Morrison was advancing. His mind was wholly engrossed by the sense of injury—injury sustained from a friend; and by the desire of vengeance on one whom be now accounted his most bitter enemy. The treasured ideas of self-importance and self-opinion—of ideal birth and quality, had become more precious to him, (like the hoard to the miser,) because he could only enjoy them in secret. But that hoard was pillaged, the idols which he had secretly worshipped had been desecrated and profaned. Insulted, abused, and beaten, he was no longer worthy, in his own opinion, of the name he bore, or the lineage which he belonged to—nothing was left to him—nothing but revenge; and as the reflection added a galling spur to every step, he determined it should be as sudden and signal as the offence.

When Robin Oig left the door of the alehouse, seven or eight English miles at least lay betwixt Morrison and him. The advance of the former was slow, limited by the sluggish pace of his cattle; the last left behind him stubble-field and hedge-row, crag and dark heath, all glittering with frost-rime in the broad November moonlight, at the rate of six miles an hour. And now the distant lowing of Morrison's cattle is heard; and now they are seen creeping like moles in size and slowness of motion on the broad face of the moor; and now he meets them—passes them, and stops their conductor.

'May good betide us,' said the Southlander—'Is this you, Robin M'Combich, or your wraith?'

'It is Robin Oig M'Combich,' answered the Highlander, 'and it is not.—But never mind that, put pe giving me the skene-dhu.'

'What! you are for back to the Highlands—The devil!—Have you selt all off before the fair? This beats all for quick markets!'

'I have not sold—I am not going north—May pe I will never go north again.—Give me pack my dirk, Hugh Morrison, or there will pe words petween us.'

'Indeed, Robin, I'll be better advised before I gie it back to you—it is a wanchancy weapon in a Highlandman's hand, and I am thinking you will be about some barns-breaking.'

'Prutt, trutt! let me have my weapon,' said Robin Oig impatiently.

'Hooly and fairly,' said his well-meaning friend. 'I'll tell you what will do better than these dirking doings—Ye ken Highlander, and Lowlander, and Border-men, are a' ae man's bairns when you are over the Scots dyke. See, the Eskdale callants, and fighting Charlie of Liddesdale, and the Lockerby lads, and the four Dandies of Lustruther, and a wheen mair grey plaids, are coming up behind; and if you are wronged, there is the hand of a Manly Morrison, we'll see you righted, if Carlisle and Stanwix baith took up the feud.'"

'To tell you the truth,' said Robin Oig, desirous of eluding the suspicions of his friend, 'I have enlisted with a party of the Black Watch, and must march off to-morrow morning.'

'Enlisted! Were you mad or drunk?—You must buy yourself off—I can lend you twenty notes, and twenty to that, if the drove sell.'

'I thank you—thank ye, Hughie; but I go with good will the gate that I am going,—so the dirk—the dirk!'

'There it is for you then, since less wunna serve. But think on what I was saying.—Waes me, it will be sair news in the braes of Balquidder, that Robin Oig M'Combich should have run an ill gate, and ta'en on.'

'Ill news in Balquidder, indeed!' echoed poor Robin: 'but Cot speed you, Hughie, and send you good marcats. Ye winna meet with Robin Oig again, either at tryste or fair.'

So saying, he shook hastily the hand of his acquaintance,

and set out in the direction from which he had advanced, with the spirit of his former pace.

'There is something wrong with the lad,' muttered the Morrison to himself; 'but we will maybe see better into it the morn's morning.'

But long ere the morning dawned, the catastrophe of our tale had taken place. It was two hours after the affray had happened, and it was totally forgotten by almost every one, when Robin Oig returned to Heskett's inn. The place was filled at once by various sorts of men, and with noises corresponding to their character. There were the grave low sounds of men engaged in busy traffic, with the laugh, the song, and the riotous jest of those who had nothing to do but to enjoy themselves. Among the last was Harry Wakefield, who, amidst a grinning group of smock-frocks, hobnailed shoes, and jolly English physiognomies, was trolling forth the old ditty,

'What though my name be Roger, Who drives the slough and cart—' when he was interrupted by a well-known voice saying in a high and stern voice, marked by the sharp Highland accent, 'Harry Waakfelt—if you be a man stand up!'

'What is the matter?—what is it?' the guests demanded of each other.

'It is only a d—d Scotsman,' said Fleecebumpkin, who was by this time very drunk, 'whom Harry Wakefield helped to his broth to-day, who is now come to have his cauld kail het again.'

'Harry Waakfelt,' repeated the same ominous summons, 'stand up, if you be a man!'

There is something in the tone of deep and concentrated passion, which attracts attention and imposes awe, even by the very sound. The guests shrunk back on every side, and gazed at the Highlander as he stood in the middle of them, his brows bent, and his features rigid with resolution.

'I will stand up with all my heart, Robin, my boy, but it shall be to shake hands with you, and drink down all unkindness. It is not the fault of your heart, man, that you don't know how to clench your hands.'

By this time he stood opposite to his antagonist; his open and unsuspecting look strangely contrasted with the stern purpose, which gleamed wild, dark, and vindictive in the eyes of the Highlander.

'Tis not thy fault, man, that, not having the luck to be an Englishman, thou canst not fight more than a school-girl.'

'I *can* fight,' answered Robin Oig sternly, but calmly, 'and you shall know it. You, Harry Waakfelt, showed me to-day how the Saxon churls fight—I show you now how the Highland Dunniewassel fights.'

He seconded the word with the action, and plunged the dagger, which he suddenly displayed, into the broad breast of the English yeoman, with such fatal certainty and force, that the hilt made a hollow sound against the breast-bone, and the double-edged point split the very heart of his victim. Harry Wakefield fell and expired with a single groan. His assassin next seized the bailiff by the collar, and offered the bloody poniard to his throat, whilst dread and surprise rendered the man incapable of defence.

'It were very just to lay you beside him,' he said, 'but the blood of a base pick-thank shall never mix on my father's dirk, with that of a brave man.'

As he spoke, he cast the man from him with so much force that he fell on the floor, while Robin, with his other hand, threw the fatal weapon into the blazing turf-fire.

'There,' he said, 'take me who likes—and let fire cleanse blood if it can.'

The pause of astonishment still continuing, Robin Oig asked for a peace-officer, and a constable having stepped out, he surrendered himself to his custody.

'A bloody night's work you have made of it,' said the constable.

'Your own fault,' said the Highlander. 'Had you kept his hands off me twa hours since, he would have been now as well and merry as he was twa minutes since.'

'It must be sorely answered,' said the peace-officer.

'Never you mind that—death pays all debts; it will pay that too.'

The horror of the bystanders began now to give way to indignation; and the sight of a favourite companion murdered in the midst of them, the provocation being, in their opinion, so utterly inadequate to the excess of vengeance, might have induced them to kill the perpetrator of the deed even upon the very spot. The constable, however, did his duty on this occasion, and with the assistance of some of the more reasonable persons present, procured horses to guard the prisoner to Carlisle, to abide his doom at the next assizes. While the escort was preparing, the prisoner neither expressed the least interest, nor attempted the slightest reply. Only, before he was carried from the fatal apartment, he desired to look at the dead body, which, raised from the floor, had been deposited upon the large table, (at the head of which Harry Wakefield had presided but a few minutes before, full of life, vigour, and animation,) until the surgeons should examine the mortal wound. The face of the corpse was decently covered with a napkin. To the surprise and horror of the bystanders, which displayed itself in a general *Ah!* drawn through clenched teeth and half-shut lips, Robin Oig removed the cloth, and gazed with a mournful but steady eye on the lifeless visage, which had been so lately animated, that the smile of good-humoured confidence in his own strength, of conciliation at once, and contempt towards his enemy, still curled his lip. While those present expected that the wound, which had so lately flooded the apartment with gore, would send forth fresh streams at the touch of the homicide, Robin Oig replaced the covering with the brief exclamation—'He was a pretty man!'

My story is nearly ended. The unfortunate Highlander stood his trial at Carlisle. I was myself present, and as a young Scottish lawyer, or barrister at least, and reputed a man of some quality, the politeness of the Sheriff of Cumberland offered me a place on the bench. The facts of the case were proved in the manner I have related them; and whatever might be at first the prejudice of the audience against a crime so un-English as that of assassination from revenge, yet when the rooted national prejudices of the prisoner had been explained, which made him consider himself as stained with indelible dishonour, when subjected to personal violence; when his previous patience, moderation, and endurance, were considered, the generosity of the English audience was inclined to regard his crime as the wayward aberration of a false idea of honour rather than as flowing from a heart naturally savage, or perverted by habitual vice. I shall never forget the charge of the venerable Judge to the jury, although not at that time liable to be much affected either by that which was eloquent or pathetic.

'We have had,' he said, 'in the previous part of our duty,' (alluding to some former trials,) 'to discuss crimes which infer disgust and abhorrence, while they call down the well-merited vengeance of the law. It is now our still more melancholy task to apply its salutary though severe enactments to a case of a very singular character, in which the crime (for a crime it is, and a deep one) arose less out of the malevolence of the heart, than the error of the understanding—less from any idea of committing wrong, than from an unhappily perverted notion of that which is right. Here we have two men, highly esteemed, it has been stated, in their rank of life, and attached, it seems, to each other as friends, one of whose lives has been already sacrificed to a punctilio, and the other is about to prove the vengeance of the offended laws; and yet both may claim our commiseration at least, as men acting in ignorance of each other's national prejudices, and unhappily misguided rather than voluntarily erring from the path of right conduct.

'In the original cause of the misunderstanding, we must in justice give the right to the prisoner at the bar. He had acquired possession of the enclosure, which was the object of competition, by a legal contract with the proprietor Mr Ireby; and yet, when accosted with reproaches undeserved in themselves, and galling doubtless to a temper at least sufficiently susceptible of passion, he offered notwithstanding to yield up half his acquisition, for the sake of peace and good neighbourhood, and his amicable proposal was rejected with scorn. Then follows the scene at Mr Heskett the publican's, and you will observe how the stranger was treated by the deceased, and, I am sorry to observe, by those around, who seem to have urged him in a manner which was aggravating in the highest degree. While he asked for peace and for composition, and offered submission to a magistrate, or to a mutual arbiter, the prisoner was insulted by a whole company, who seem on this occasion to have forgotten the national maxim of 'fair play;' and while attempting to escape from the place in peace, he was intercepted, struck down, and beaten to the effusion of his blood.

'Gentlemen of the Jury, it was with some impatience that I heard my learned brother, who opened the case for the crown, give an unfavourable turn to the prisoner's conduct on this occasion. He said the prisoner was afraid to encounter his antagonist in fair fight, or to submit to the laws of the ring; and that therefore, like a cowardly Italian, he had recourse to his fatal stiletto, to murder the man whom he dared not meet in manly encounter. I observed the prisoner shrink from this part of the accusation with the abhorrence natural to a brave man;

and as I would wish to make my words impressive, when I point his real crime, I must secure his opinion of my impartiality, by rebutting every thing that seems to me a false accusation. There can be no doubt that the prisoner is a man of resolution—too much resolution—I wish to Heaven that he had less, or rather that he had had a better education to regulate it.

'Gentlemen, as to the laws my brother talks of, they may be known in the Bull-ring, or the Bear-garden, or the Cockpit, but they are not known here. Or, if they should be so far admitted as furnishing a species of proof that no malice was intended in this sort of combat, from which fatal accidents do sometimes arise, it can only be so admitted when both parties are *in pari casu*, equally acquainted with, and equally willing to refer themselves to, that species of arbitrement. But will it be contended that a man of superior rank and education is to be subjected, or is obliged to subject himself, to this coarse and brutal strife, perhaps in opposition to a younger, stronger, or more skilful opponent? Certainly even the pugilistic code, if founded upon the fair play of Merry Old England, as my brother alleges it to be, can contain nothing so preposterous. And, gentlemen of the jury, if the laws would support an English gentleman, wearing, we will suppose, his sword, in defending himself by force against a violent personal aggression of the nature offered to this prisoner, they will not less protect a foreigner and a stranger, involved in the same unpleasing circumstances. If, therefore, gentlemen of the jury, when thus pressed by a *vis major*, the object of obloquy to a whole company, and of direct violence from one at least, and, as he might reasonably apprehend, from more, the panel had produced the weapon which his countrymen, as we are informed, generally carry about their persons, and the same unhappy circumstance had ensued which you have heard detailed in evidence, I could not in my conscience have asked from you a verdict of murder.

The prisoner's personal defence might indeed, even in that case, have gone more or less beyond the *Moderamen inculpatae tutelae*, spoken of by lawyers, but the punishment incurred would have been that of manslaughter, not of murder. I beg leave to add, that I should have thought this milder species of charge was demanded in the case supposed, notwithstanding the statute of James I. cap. 8, which takes the case of slaughter by stabbing with a short weapon, even without malice prepense, out of the benefit of clergy. For this statute of stabbing, as it is termed, arose out of a temporary cause; and as the real guilt is the same, whether the slaughter be committed by the dagger, or by sword or pistol, the benignity of the modern law places them all on the same, or nearly the same footing.

'But, gentlemen of the jury, the pinch of the case lies in the interval of two hours interposed betwixt the reception of the injury and the fatal retaliation. In the heat of affray and *chaude melée*, law, compassionating the infirmities of humanity, makes allowance for the passions which rule such a stormy moment— for the sense of present pain, for the apprehension of further injury, for the difficulty of ascertaining with due accuracy the precise degree of violence which is necessary to protect the person of the individual, without annoying or injuring the assailant more than is absolutely necessary. But the time necessary to walk twelve miles, however speedily performed, was an interval sufficient for the prisoner to have recollected himself; and the violence with which he carried his purpose into effect, with so many circumstances of deliberate determination, could neither be induced by the passion of anger, nor that of fear. It was the purpose and the act of predetermined revenge, for which law neither can, will, nor ought to have sympathy or allowance.

'It is true, we may repeat to ourselves, in alleviation of this poor man's unhappy action, that his case is a very peculiar one. The country which he inhabits was, in the days of many now alive, inaccessible to the laws, not only of England, which have not even yet penetrated thither, but to those to which our neighbours of Scotland are subjected, and which must be supposed to be, and no doubt actually are, founded upon the general principles of justice and equity which pervade every civilized country. Amongst their mountains, as among the North American Indians, the various tribes were wont to make war upon each other, so that each man was obliged to go armed for his own protection. These men, from the ideas which they entertained of their own descent and of their own consequence, regarded themselves as so many cavaliers or men-at-arms, rather than as the peasantry of a peaceful country. Those laws of the ring, as my brother terms them, were unknown to the race of warlike mountaineers; that decision of quarrels by no other weapons than those which nature has given every man, must to them have seemed as vulgar and as preposterous as to the Noblesse of France. Revenge, on the other hand, must have been as familiar to their habits of society as to those of the Cherokees or Mohawks. It is indeed, as described by Bacon, at bottom a kind of wild untutored justice; for the fear of retaliation must withhold the hands of the oppressor where there is no regular law to check daring violence. But though all this may be granted, and though we may allow that, such having been the case of the Highlands in the days of the prisoner's fathers, many of the opinions and sentiments must still continue to influence the present generation, it cannot, and ought not, even in this most painful case, to alter the administration of the law, either in your hands, gentlemen of the jury, or in mine. The first object of civilisation is to place the general protection of the law, equally administered, in the room of that wild justice, which every man cut and carved for himself, according to the length of his sword and the strength of his arm. The law says to the subjects, with a voice only inferior to that of the Deity, 'Vengeance is mine.' The instant that there is time for passion to cool, and reason to interpose, an injured party must become aware that the law assumes the exclusive cognisance of the right and wrong betwixt the parties, and opposes her inviolable buckler to every attempt of the private party to right himself. I repeat, that this unhappy man ought personally to be the object rather of our pity than our abhorrence, for he failed in his ignorance, and from mistaken notions of honour. But his crime is not the less that of murder, gentlemen, and, in your high and important office, it is your duty so to find. Englishmen have their angry passions as well as Scots; and should this man's action remain unpunished, you may unsheath, under various pretences, a thousand daggers betwixt the Land's-end and the Orkneys.'

The venerable Judge thus ended what, to judge by his apparent emotion, and by the tears which filled his eyes, was really a painful task. The jury, according to his instructions, brought in a verdict of Guilty; and Robin Oig M'Combich, *alias* McGregor, was sentenced to death, and left for execution, which took place accordingly. He met his fate with great firmness, and acknowledged the justice of his sentence. But he repelled indignantly the observations of those who accused him of attacking an unarmed man. 'I give a life for the life I took,' he said, 'and what can I do more?'

ABOUT TERRY O'BRIEN

Terry O'Brien is an academic with three decades of experience in teaching language and communication skills in India and abroad. He also headed a college under the auspices of the University of Delhi.

A prolific writer, with several books to his credit, Terry O'Brien is a reputed professional motivational speaker and a quizmaster.